Dear Reader,

We're thrilled that some of Harlequin's most famous families are making an encore appearance! With this special Famous Families fifty-book collection, we are proud to offer you the chance to relive the drama, the glamour, the suspense and the romance of four of Harlequin's most beloved families—the Fortunes, the Bravos, the McCabes and the Cavanaughs.

The Cavanaughs, our fourth and final family, believe in honor, justice and protecting the innocent. These values have forged a strong bond among the members of the close-knit Cavanaugh family, and make them a force to be reckoned with in the small town of Aurora, California.

The Cavanaughs do share one trait with our other famous families, though. When romance hits, all bets are off! Love changes the game for all these independent souls, turning their vulnerability into even greater strength. Prepare to be charmed by the California family created by *USA TODAY* bestselling author Marie Ferrarella.

Happy reading,

The Editors

MARIE FERRARELLA

This *USA TODAY* bestselling and RITA® Award-winning author has written more than two hundred books for Harlequin Books and Silhouette Books, some under the name Marie Nicole. Her romances are beloved by fans worldwide. Visit her website, www.marieferrarella.com.

FAMOUS FAMILIES

the CAVANAUGHS

USA TODAY Bestselling Author

MARIE FERRARELLA

In Broad Daylight

HARLEQUIN®

entertain, enrich, inspire™

To Patience,
who has a great deal.
With thanks,
Marie

Recycling programs
for this product may
not exist in your area.

ISBN-13: 978-0-373-36525-8

IN BROAD DAYLIGHT

www.Harlequin.com

Printed in U.S.A.

FAMOUS FAMILIES

The Fortunes

Cowboy at Midnight by Ann Major
A Baby Changes Everything by Marie Ferrarella
In the Arms of the Law by Peggy Moreland
Lone Star Rancher by Laurie Paige
The Good Doctor by Karen Rose Smith
The Debutante by Elizabeth Bevarly
Keeping Her Safe by Myrna Mackenzie
The Law of Attraction by Kristi Gold
Once a Rebel by Sheri WhiteFeather
Military Man by Marie Ferrarella
Fortune's Legacy by Maureen Child
The Reckoning by Christie Ridgway

The Bravos by Christine Rimmer

The Nine-Month Marriage
Marriage by Necessity
Practically Married
Married by Accident
The Millionaire She Married
The M.D. She Had to Marry
The Marriage Agreement
The Bravo Billionaire
The Marriage Conspiracy
His Executive Sweetheart
Mercury Rising
Scrooge and the Single Girl

The McCabes by Cathy Gillen Thacker

Dr. Cowboy
Wildcat Cowboy
A Cowboy's Woman
A Cowboy Kind of Daddy
A Night Worth Remembering
The Seven-Year Proposal
The Dad Next Door
The Last Virgin in Texas
Texas Vows: A McCabe Family Saga
The Ultimate Texas Bachelor
Santa's Texas Lullaby
A Texas Wedding Vow
Blame It on Texas
A Laramie, Texas Christmas
From Texas, With Love

The Cavanaughs by Marie Ferrarella

Racing Against Time
Crime and Passion
Internal Affair
Dangerous Games
The Strong Silent Type
Cavanaugh's Woman
In Broad Daylight
Alone in the Dark
Dangerous Disguise
The Woman Who Wasn't There
Cavanaugh Watch
Cavanaugh Heat

Chapter 1

There was nothing he hated worse than a kidnapping case.

The thought of someone who was part of your life suddenly vanishing without a trace—leaving you powerless to find them—had always seemed like the most heinous of crimes to Detective Dax Cavanaugh.

Maybe it was because he was acquainted firsthand with the situation. His Uncle Andrew and the family had gone through all sorts of personal hell when his Aunt Rose had vanished. It was fifteen years before they'd any answers.

The torture was in not knowing.

The torture was in the various awful, haunting scenarios that your mind could drag up despite your best efforts to block them.

In his personal opinion, Dax thought as he took a street that led him to a prestigious address, every kidnapper should be left for ten minutes with the families of the victims. That's all, just ten minutes. And then justice would be served. But he was sworn to uphold a more traditional justice and that was what was bringing him and his partner to Harwood Academy.

A tangle of two fire engines and one ambulance, each belching personnel onto the front lawn of the very private Harwood Academy less than twenty minutes ago, made finding a place to park his navy Crown Victoria a feat comparable to finding a place to stand within ten minutes of the beginning of the annual Rose Bowl Parade.

"Looks like this is the place," his partner, Nathan Brown, commented.

"Yeah, and it looks like everyone else has found it ahead of us."

Muttering a frustrated expletive, Dax brought the vehicle to a forty-three degree angle against a late model Mercedes in the small parking lot, unfolded his large frame and got out, slamming the door behind him.

Gregarious and outgoing, the eldest son of Brian Cavanaugh, chief of detectives of the Aurora, California, police department, Dax was known for his easygoing humor. But not today. Nothing sobered him faster than a kidnapping. Especially the kidnapping of a child, as this was reported to be.

He glanced toward his right, to assure himself that

Nathan had gotten out and was keeping up as he cut across the lot. Nathan was as short as he was tall and on unseasonably hot days like today, he liked to complain about his "freaky, stork-like legs." To which Dax would respond by saying something about his partner's stubby limbs.

But no such banter took place today. Because a six-year-old girl might be missing.

Dax held a good thought. It was in his nature, a special "Cavanaugh gene" that resided in about two-thirds of the family and shone like a beacon during the darkest of times.

Dax scanned the area, taking in the outer chaos quickly.

The lawn and lot were filled not only with cars and firefighters, but well-groomed, uniformed children. The last batch, coming in various shapes and heights, were being shepherded incredibly well by their teachers. There was noise and confusion everywhere. The firefighters appeared to be retreating. The emergency medical personnel, who had arrived on the tail of the second fire truck, were packing up. The opened rear doors showed Dax that they had no one to take back with them.

False alarm?

Dax sniffed the air. The smell of smoke was conspicuously absent.

"Looks like they're all dressed up with nowhere to go," he commented, looking at a team of firefighters who were retracting the hose that had ultimately not been necessary. It had been usurped, he later discovered, by a fire extinguisher.

Nathan squinted, looking toward the unharmed four-story building that housed the academy. "Kind of elaborate for a fire drill," he quipped.

"This was no drill," Dax commented.

The children, he'd noted, seemed more excited than frightened. He remembered the monotony of his own school days. An honest-to-gosh fire would have been more than welcomed to break up the tedium that marked his less than auspicious elementary career. He hadn't figured out that he liked learning until somewhere midway through high school.

He wouldn't have fit in here, Dax judged as he and Nathan picked their way through the pint-sized throng. These were the children of the wealthy.

Wealth came in all sorts of forms. In his family wealth was the amount of love available at any given moment of the day or night. Dollars, at times, had to be stretched, but love never was.

Even for him. And he had been a wild one, turning his late mother's dark hair gray way before its time, he thought fondly.

One pint-sized student stood directly in his path, looking up at him as if he were a giant oak tree. Curiosity was imprinted on the boy's face. Dax gave him an obligatory smile and stepped to one side.

"What do you think it costs to send your kid here?" Nathan asked, raising his voice to be heard above the commotion.

Nathan had three kids, all of whom were under the age of twelve. Remembering his own household with its rabble of four, Dax figured Nathan's wife had sainthood pretty much under wraps.

He laughed dryly at his partner's innocent question. "More than you and I make in a year, buddy."

Nathan blew out a breath and nodded. The academy, established some fifty years ago by the grandfather of the present headmaster, had been the first place of learning for some of the present captains of industry, both within the world of business and in the entertainment world. If rumors he'd picked up were true, a couple of senators had emerged from these halls as well.

"Hey, the public school system's not all that bad," Dax pointed out. "You and I went through it and we turned out pretty good."

Nathan spared him a long look. "Well, at least one of us did." Suddenly, the shorter man was alert, spotting the person he figured they were both looking for. "Nine o'clock," Nathan nodded in that general direction. "Looks like that might be the guy who runs the place."

Dax was already changing direction. "He's not a 'guy,' Brown, he's the headmaster. See, that's why your kid'll never go here."

"Yeah, that and the fact that I'm short a hundred-thousand dollars for the tab." Nathan sighed. He tried to match Dax's stride as the latter lengthened his. "Damn it," he barked, lowering his voice again because of the children who appeared to be everywhere, "slow down, Icabod."

Dax grinned at the jive. He bore about as much resemblance to the Washington Irving character as a sunset bore to a light bulb. Tall, broad-shouldered, with a small waist that came from more than a passing acquaintance with the department's gym, Dax had his mother's emerald-green eyes and his father's black hair, quick smile and chiseled features.

Women, much to his partner's wistful envy, threw themselves at Dax. He was good at catching them, then setting them down. Life was too unsettled for the kind of long-term commitment a relationship would have asked of him. Besides, he was enjoying himself and in no hurry to have that part of his life over. If he felt the need for family, hell, there were his siblings and his cousins to turn to. At last count, the younger Cavanaughs numbered eleven. There was always family to spare as far as he was concerned.

Nathan checked his pocket for his pad. "Think this was all a mistake, like the fire?"

Dax shook his head. "No."

The expressions he observed on the teachers' faces looked too worried, too concerned. It went beyond just trying to keep track of the children closest to them until they were herded back into the building and their classrooms.

Just before he reached the headmaster, a stately looking man whose iron-gray hair made him appear older than his chronological years, a young woman got into his line of vision.

The instant she did, his eyes were locked on her.

For a second Dax almost forgot to breathe; she was that startlingly beautiful. The kind of beautiful he would have fully expected to see on the cover of one of those magazines that populated the checkout area of his local supermarket. The kind of beautiful he wouldn't have believed was real, or could be achieved without a great deal of powder and paint; both of which would have been visible in person.

Except it wasn't. The young woman before him with the spun-gold hair appeared to be all fresh-faced and natural.

As air returned to his lungs, he felt his pulse quickening the way it did whenever he was confronted with a life or death situation. But this was neither. Gorgeous or not, she was just another person who was there, he reminded himself.

And he had a job to do. There was a little girl who was presently unaccounted for.

"Mr. Harwood?" Dax's deep voice cut through the din as easily as a sword cut through butter.

Matthew Harwood looked away from the young woman he was talking to, proper concern etched with stately precision on his square face. He looked weary as well as wary.

"Yes?"

"I'm Detective Cavanaugh, this is Detective Brown," Dax nodded behind him, doing his best to ignore the woman on Harwood's left. "You reported a missing little girl."

"I reported it," the woman who had altered his breathing pattern responded before Harwood could say anything. "Her name is Annie Tyler and she's in my class."

Which placed her in the first round of questioning. He'd hit a jackpot at a time when he couldn't afford to be distracted, Dax thought. And if ever there was a woman who was distracting, this was one.

Nodding at the information, he looked around. "Is there somewhere where we can go and talk? Somewhere a little less noisy?" he asked.

As if second-guessing him, Harwood was already waving over an aid. "Mrs. Miller, could you take over Mrs. York's class?"

Mrs. York.

She was married.

Droplets of disappointment, materializing out of nowhere, rained over him. But maybe it was better this way. He was good at perpetually keeping several balls in the air at the same time, but the law of averages was against him. Someday, one of those balls was going to drop and he couldn't allow for it to be one associated with his work. He loved being a cop, loved making a difference. Loved the rush when a crime was finally solved, or a perpetrator was brought to justice.

Or a child was recovered, he underscored. That meant focusing exclusively on the job.

Focused or not, glancing at the woman's hand seemed only natural.

There was no ring on the appropriate finger.

Widowed?

Divorced?

Not his concern, the same harsh voice that had long ago been assigned the role of his personal devil's advocate whispered within him.

Mrs. Miller was a pleasant-faced, full-figured woman who radiated enthusiasm and sunshine as she approached. She also radiated concern as her eyes shifted to the blonde. "Oh, I hope we find her."

We. As if they'd somehow misplaced the child. Was the little girl given to pranks? To disappearing from sight, only to watch from a secret hiding place as pandemonium ensued? Was this a bid for attention? So many of these kids hardly cohabited with their parents at all and were desperate for attention.

"I'm sorry, you are…?" Nathan was asking the blonde before he could.

"Brenda York." Brenda put out her hand. When Dax took it, he thought it felt icy. As if she was worried. Or afraid. "I teach first grade.

His own first grade teacher had been a Mrs. Flack, a short, squat woman with bottle-orange hair. She'd favored shapeless smocks, sensible dark brown shoes and smelled of peppermint because she always seemed to be sucking on the candy, something her students, unfairly he thought, weren't allowed to do. Had Mrs. Flack looked remotely like Brenda York, he might have discovered the pleasure of learning a lot earlier than in high school.

"This way," Harwood directed, pointing toward the front entrance.

Behind them, the last of the firefighters were getting onto a truck. The first truck had already pulled away. The din that had been humming since before their arrival was gradually fading into the warm May air. It amazed Dax how quickly order was restored. Each and every student seemed aware that it was time to go back to the world they had vacated for such a brief amount of time. The excitement of the fire, real or imagined, was over. The teachers had obviously done their level best to keep the news of the possible abduction from spreading and reaching any young ears.

Dax glanced over his shoulder, watching the students as they resumed a tight formation before they literally marched back into the building.

Hushed whispers hummed in the air like june bugs, all, he guessed, centering around his and Nathan's recent arrival. He returned one child's gaze and smiled before turning back around.

His eyes met Brenda's completely by accident. Hers were a deep crystal blue. Intense, shining like two blue lights, they seemed to penetrate his very soul. He could have sworn there was some kind of electrical shock that had gone through him.

She lowered her eyes and turned back away.

Dax felt like a survivor of a train wreck who hadn't

been aware that the train had even gone off course until the impact had hit.

Behind him, Nathan stood up on his toes. "One step at a time, buddy, one step at a time."

He gave Nathan a dirty look. Nathan gave him a knowing one.

They entered the building. The floors were polished to a high sheen, but were amazingly non-slippery. Lawsuits obviously were the scourge of even a place like Harwood. Well-cared for wooden doors lined both sides of the corridor like timeless, learned sentries. The headmaster brought them to the far end of the hall.

"We can talk in here," Harwood was saying.

Opening a door, he led them into a somber room whose walls were lined from floor to ceiling with books. The only break in the decor were two windows that somehow managed to filter out the light and allowed only gloom into the medium-sized room, and the door which seemed to shyly claim a space amid massive bookshelves.

Once the door was closed behind them, all noise, soft or otherwise, from the outside world ceased to exist. For a moment, the only sounds evident were the individual breaths that they took.

It was a room designed for intimidation, Dax thought. Any kid who was called in here was already scared out of his or her mind. He exchanged looks with Nathan and could tell that the same thought had crossed his partner's mind as well.

Rather than stand with them, the headmaster took his place behind the massive desk; whether to demarcate his position or to keep himself separated from the situation, Dax didn't know, but it came across as a definite power play of some sort.

The teacher, he noted, remained with him and his partner. Joining ranks? Or infiltrating the enemy?

She smelled of jasmine, or maybe gardenias. He never could get things like flowers straight. To him, a flower was a flower. But the scent, well, that was pretty unnerving right now.

For the first time in his life, he wished he had a cold, or some kind of allergy that would have blocked his nasal capacity. He found the scent seductive.

Just like the woman.

Brenda York appeared agitated, he noted. Was that natural concern on her part? Or was there something else at play here? He had too little input to go on and his gut was otherwise occupied, giving him no clue.

The thing that sometimes bothered him about his chosen way of life was that he could never look at anything simply. Everything had two sides and, like as not, multi-layers that usually needed unraveling. It made simplicity a thing of the past and an unattainable dream these days.

Harwood cleared his throat. But right now, Dax was more interested in what Brenda York had to say. He turned toward her, the action blocking out the headmaster.

"Are you the one who first noticed she was missing?" Dax asked her.

She still couldn't believe any of this was happening. It was like a nightmare, a horrible, horrible nightmare and she was waiting to wake up. Except that she was already awake.

Calm, you have to stay calm. You can't help Annie if you're not calm.

She realized she was clenching her hands at her sides, digging her nails into her palms. She forced herself to open them. "Yes."

The single word sounded tortured to Dax. An act? The truth? For the time being, he gave her the benefit of the doubt as he began to ask his questions. Out of the corner of his eye, he saw Nathan take out his pad. Nathan believed in writing everything down. As for him, he kept all the notes in his head. He'd always had that ability, to go into the recesses of his mind and pluck out whatever tiny fact he needed whenever he needed it.

He watched her face, looking for any telltale sign that might give him a clue as to what she was thinking, what she was really feeling. "Are you sure she's missing? Maybe she wandered in with another group of kids. I saw a lot of activity going on when we pulled up—"

This time, Harwood was the one who cut in. "Our children are taught discipline from the very first day they come to Harwood Academy," he informed Dax with alacrity. "They do not wander."

Dax couldn't tell if the man was taking offense on behalf of his students, or if he felt that anything other than perfect behavior reflected badly on him.

In complete control of the situation, Dax lifted a shoulder and carelessly let it fall again. "Yeah, but kids are still kids. There's all this noise and excitement going on, firefighters, trucks, ambulances—"

"Ambulance," Harwood corrected automatically. "There was only one."

Dax inclined his head. The man was a stickler, he thought. Possibly a little obsessive. He was grateful that his parents hadn't had the money to send him to a private school.

"Ambulance," he allowed. "With all this confusion, she might have taken the opportunity to duck out on you and get in with one of her friends."

If only, Brenda thought. If only.

But she'd searched the area, asking all the children who might have seen her if they had. Each time, she'd gotten a shake of the head in response. The tiny mouse of a child, who reminded her so much of herself at that age, was nowhere to be found.

"That's just it," Brenda told him, her voice growing a little more firm with every word she uttered, "Annie doesn't really have any friends."

There was a glimmer of pain in her eyes as she told him that. Dax couldn't help wondering if it was genuine, or if he'd been confronted with a very good actress. It certainly wouldn't have been the first time a kidnapper had tried to put something over on him.

And until proven otherwise, he had to think of her that way. As someone who might somehow be involved in the kidnapping, if that was what it actually was. After all, Annie Tyler was last seen in her care.

Glancing at Nathan before continuing, Dax crossed his arms before him. A full moment went by before he spoke again. Time, his father had told him early in his career, was both their friend and their enemy. The more time that went by, the less likely a missing child was to be found. But if you gave a guilty person who wasn't a hardened criminal enough time, they tended to say or do something to incriminate themselves.

Dax studied the blond woman before him, trying not to notice that, even though she was wearing a lavender two-piece suit, the killer figure she possessed was more than evident. He motioned her toward a seat, but she shook her head, obviously preferring to stand.

Or refusing to be placed in the position of having someone stand over her.

He placed himself so that he could easily look at both her and the headmaster. "All right, Mrs. York, why don't you tell us exactly what happened. And start at the beginning. Before the fire trucks." He watched her chest rise as she take in a deep breath. Steeling himself off, he forced his eyes to her face. "Take your time," he counseled quietly. "And don't leave anything out."

Chapter 2

Her mind felt as if it were completely jumbled up, with all the thoughts glued together in one giant ball. Brenda strove to peel apart the layers, arranging the events of the last hour in their proper sequence.

Because she didn't begin immediately, Dax fired a question at her. Patience, when it came to cases, had never been his strong suit. The few times he had been assigned to a stakeout, he had all but climbed up one side of the wall and down the other.

"Let's begin with the fire." He pinned her with a look. "Was there an actual fire?" He hadn't smelled any smoke entering the building, but something or someone had to have set off the alarm.

As if riding to her rescue, Harwood drew himself up behind his desk.

"Yes, there was," he cut in. "A small one." He glanced at Brenda before adding, "The fire chief told me that some papers in a wastepaper basket had caught fire. They used one of our fire extinguishers to put it out. It turned out simpler that way."

Dax exchanged looks with Nathan. Wastepaper baskets didn't just spontaneously combust. "That sounds as if it might have been deliberately set." His gaze swept over Brenda before returning to the headmaster. "Are any of your kids budding pyromaniacs or overly fascinated with matches?"

Brenda's eyes widened at the suggestion. "No!" she snapped. Some of her pupils were starved for attention and might on occasion act out, but they were five- and six-years-old and that kind of behavior was only normal.

Harwood was sputtering indignantly. "I assure you that my school—"

Dax waved his hand in a downward motion, as if banking down their protests.

"Just a question," he told them mildly, although he had posed it to see both of their reactions. The woman was protective while the headmaster came off as concerned about his school's reputation. "Would anyone else have set the fire?"

Nathan raised an eyebrow, looking up from the notes he was religiously scribbling down. "You're thinking maybe it was a diversion?"

Dax nodded.

So had she, the moment she'd overheard the fire

chief telling Matthew Harwood that the origin of the fire had been found in her wastepaper basket. A diversion to take attention away from the fact that Annie Tyler was being stolen.

The very thought ate away at her. She should have realized something was wrong. There was no earthly reason why, but somehow, her instincts should have told her that something was wrong.

She might as well tell him before he found out on his own. "It was my wastepaper basket."

Her student, her wastepaper basket. Dax looked at the woman with deepening interest. It seemed too simple, but then, most criminals were not the masterminds that so frequently populated the more intriguing mysteries and action movies. Wanting to race, he still took it one step at a time.

Facing her, his back blocking out Harwood, he asked, "Were you in the room at the time?"

She could almost sense what he was thinking. Brenda took a breath and shook her head. "No. The class and I were giving a tour to Mr. and Mrs. Kingsley—"

She saw the good-looking detective's eyes narrow just a little, as if he was filtering in this new information. "Who?"

"Parents of a prospective new student," Harwood explained, moving so that Dax could see him. The man looked none-too-happy about being ignored. "It's done all the time."

That didn't sound quite right to him. In his experience, teachers were all too happy to escape from their classroom for a few minutes, leaving a slightly more mature child in charge of the class for the duration of their absence.

"Taking your whole class out?" Dax asked in disbelief, waiting to be corrected.

No such correction came. "It's to show how well-behaved our students are," Harwood told him. "We're quite proud of that."

The detective still didn't look as if he believed them. Brenda felt a spark of resentment building. She knew he was just doing his job, but she couldn't help feeling that he was wasting precious time with these trivial details.

"The students each take turns telling the parents about the different activities we have here at Harwood." She enumerated some of the highlights. "There's a little theater group, an art room, things the regular schools cut back on."

His face never changed expression as he listened to her description. She liked the shorter detective better, she thought. At least Detective Brown looked compassionate.

"And where was Annie during this show-and-tell process?" the suspicious detective asked.

In her mind's eye, she could see the little girl. Annie had begun at the head of the group but with each step taken, she kept drifting toward the rear of the line. Strangers always affected her that way; made her even shyer than she was.

"She was hanging back."

The poker face remained. "And you didn't coax her forward?"

Was that suspicion she heard in his voice? Did he actually think she'd do anything to harm any of the children, especially Annie? Just what kind of a monster did he think she was? Fueled by guilt, it took effort to bank down her anger. "I was just about to do that when the alarm went off."

"And then what?"

She'd heard the alarm just as they'd left the art room. She remembered feeling a sense of panic. The idea of a fire spreading through the school had always horrified her. Because of that, she had been the one to suggest to Matthew that they double the amount of fire drills performed. "And then I made sure that I got my class outside the building."

Dax deliberately moved into her space, crowding her. "You didn't stop to count heads?"

Her eyes narrowed. "No, not until we were all outside the building."

"And then you counted heads."

Brenda could feel her temper unraveling as guilt danced around it. She should have kept Annie with her. But she could remember how painful it was at times not to be able to just shrink away, to hang back. Annie had been making progress, opening up a little, but there'd been a relapse in the last few days and she'd been trying to get at the source of it without much success.

So she'd tried not to push too hard and then this had happened.

Brenda raised her chin up as if she were silently showing him she was up to any challenge he was throwing her way.

His sister did that move, Dax thought. Just before she lit into him.

"Yes," the teacher responded between clenched teeth, "then I counted heads."

Nathan looked up from the notes he was taking. "When you saw she was missing, what did you do?"

There had been no hesitation on her part. "I ran back into the building."

As if he felt he had to vouch for her actions, Harwood interjected, "One of the firefighters attempted to stop her, but she went right around him."

Nathan smiled at her before resuming his notes. "Brave lady."

Stubborn would have been the way he'd have put it, Dax thought. He was well-acquainted with stubborn. His family, especially the female portion of it, had a patent on the emotion.

Brenda shrugged off the praise. Bravery had nothing to do with it.

"I had no idea where the fire was or how bad it was. I was just worried that Annie might have run back to the classroom." She saw the silent question in the taller detective's eyes and explained. "She has this stuffed animal she keeps in her desk, a rabbit." It had taken more than a week of coaxing before Annie had told her about the rabbit. It had been a gift from her father and she clung to it whenever she missed him and wanted him close. "I thought she might have gone back for it."

Dax never took his eyes from her face. "But she didn't?"

Brenda shook her head. "She wasn't there."

"Was the rabbit?"

The question caught her short. "I didn't think to check." There had been a fireman in the room. He'd just finished putting out the fire and there was water everywhere. Water, smoke, but no Annie. "Why, was that important?"

At this point, until things were ruled out, everything was important. "It might be. If it's missing, then she either took it herself, or someone who knew about her attachment to it took the rabbit to try to use it to lure her away." He paused for a moment as the words sank in, trying not to allow the distress he saw in the woman's eyes to get to him. He couldn't afford to have his sympathies, or anything else, get in the way so that it impaired his judgment. "Where are these Kingsleys now?" he asked.

Harwood stepped in to field the question. "They left soon after the alarm went off, right after we evacuated the building. Said they'd be back when things were calmer." His tone told Dax that the man didn't hold out much hope that they would return.

He looked from Brenda to Harwood. "And they left together."

"Yes," Harwood answered.

Dax shifted his eyes toward the woman. "Were they together all the time?"

Brenda thought for a moment, but her mind still felt as if it was wrapped up in cotton batting. Some events were sharp, others that took place almost at the same time were hazy.

"I think so." She bit her lip, hating this, hating the fact that she felt so shaky. She looked at him helplessly. "I'm not sure."

Dax's expression remained stony. "Think about it," he advised.

All right, she wasn't imagining it. He did suspect her. But why? Because the fire had started in her room? Because Annie was her student? Or because he was one of those gung ho policemen who wanted to clear his caseload and it didn't matter to him if he had the right person or not?

Either way, she wasn't about to let this continue. If he suspected her, he wouldn't take anything she said at face value and that could only impede finding Annie.

Shutting down the host of emotions bouncing wildly around inside of her, Brenda raised her head and looked him squarely in the eye. "Are you inferring that I had something to do with this?"

Dax took the opportunity to play along with the lead she gave him. "Did you?"

Thinking he suspected her was one thing, having him almost come out and say it was another. The reality of it cut through her like a saber, drawing blood and indignation.

"No! I would never—"

He raised his hand, silencing her with a single motion. He had no time for theatrics. For the time being, he'd buy into her innocence.

"Then let's continue." Dax turned toward Harwood. The man's complexion was almost ashen. The headline Teacher Involved in Student's Kidnapping had probably flashed through the headmaster's mind, Dax mused. "And you're sure she's not around anywhere. Did someone check the other classrooms?"

Had his suspicions clogged his ears? "I already checked the other classrooms—" Brenda began. That was why the police had been called in to begin with.

"But not everywhere," Nathan gently pointed out.

Dax thought of his own unruly elementary school experience. There were coat rooms and closets and a basement that probably ran the length of the school. A kid could hide anywhere. He had on more than one occasion. The sixth-grade coat room was where he'd stolen his first kiss from Amanda Jackson.

Brenda blew out a breath. "No, not everywhere," she agreed.

"The students are all returning to their rooms," Harwood pointed out. Had the door to his office been opened, the sound of shuffling feet would have been evident. "The teachers would notice someone who didn't belong in their room. We keep the class sizes quite small."

"Besides," Brenda felt compelled to insist again, defending the little girl who couldn't defend herself,

"Annie wouldn't do that. Annie was just beginning to come out of her shell, she wouldn't deliberately run off or hide."

"Shell?" Dax left the word hanging in the air, waiting for her to elaborate.

Oh Annie, I hope you're not too scared. Brenda struggled not to let her empathy get the better of her. Annie had to be so frightened right now.

"Annie was—is," she amended because the condition still held the little girl fast, "painfully shy, insecure. She's an only child. Her father's the film director Simon Tyler and her mother is an actress, or was. Rebecca Allen-Tyler. Supposedly, she's retired now, but she's still always off somewhere, away from Annie. They both usually are." She knew that Simon was in Europe, directing a movie and Annie's mother was somewhere in New York, on a shopping spree and visiting friends. Annie had shared that with her just this morning.

He wasn't familiar with the woman's name, but he did recognize the girl's father. Dax didn't know much about movies, leaving that to the film enthusiasts in the family. However, even he knew who Simon Tyler was. Anyone who ever walked into a blockbuster movie in the last ten years was familiar with Simon Tyler. His name appeared above only the highest moneymakers.

"So who takes care of her?" he asked Brenda, since she seemed to be the expert here.

An image of Annie, her eyes huge and sad, flashed

through her mind. "The housekeeper for the most part," Brenda told him.

Dax studied her again, trying to view her as an integral part of the scenario instead of quite possibly the most stunning woman he'd ever seen. "You seem to know a lot about her. You take that much of an interest in all your students?"

There it was again, that suspicion. She knew he was doing his job, but she didn't have to like it. "Yes, I do. But Annie is special."

"Special how?" Dax prodded.

"She's very intelligent," Harwood said. It was evident that he disliked being ignored.

Nathan flipped to yet another clean page. "Doogie Howser intelligent?"

Dax looked at his partner as if the latter had just lapsed into a foreign language. "Who?"

Nathan gave him a patronizing grin. TV trivia was the one area that he had covered while Dax wandered through it like a newborn babe. "I'll explain it in the car," Nathan promised.

"Gifted," Brenda explained for his benefit. "And yes, I think she was."

She didn't add that she related to the little girl on almost all levels. Annie felt isolated from her parents and so had she. But in her own case, it was a physically and verbally abusive father who had caused the chasm that existed between she and her parents.

Until she left both of them, her mother had been no help, no buffer against her father's volatile temper. Two days before her ninth birthday, she'd come home to find a note from her mother in the kitchen, addressed to her. The note said that she couldn't take it any longer and that she was leaving in search of what she knew had to be a better life.

The memory shivered up and down her spine now, all these years later. Her father had beaten her when she'd told him the contents of the note.

At eighteen, she'd taken her mother's cue and left home for good, marrying Wade York not because she was in love with him, but because she loved him for being everything her father was not. Eventually, she'd come to learn that loving someone for lack of certain qualities wasn't enough. After seven years of trying, she and Wade had drifted apart.

In addition to the feeling of isolation, she'd related to the shy, withdrawn girl with the golden hair on another plane. Annie had been tested at near genius level, the same level that she herself had attained. In her case, there had been no one to push her; no one to help her make use of her potential; no teacher who had seen the spark. She'd been left on her own to discover it, finally enrolling in college while her husband, a marine, was shipped from one end of the globe to the other.

Brenda was determined that Annie was not going to fall by the wayside as she had.

But now Annie was missing. And it was her fault. She'd failed the girl.

Dax stepped back to open the door leading out of

Harwood's office. "Why don't we go back to your classroom?"

"All right." She squared her shoulders and pushing past him, she took the lead.

Once out in the hallway, Harwood was quick to catch up to her. "No one blames you for this, Brenda," he said in a hushed tone.

Her anger, directed against both the brash detective and herself, softened slightly as she turned toward the man who had been nothing but kind to her. The man who, she knew if she'd give him a chance, would have been ready and eager to be more to her than just the man who signed her paychecks.

But despite the fact that he was a highly educated headmaster and Wade had been a marine who'd entered the service before he'd graduated high school, Matthew Harwood was too much like Wade for her. The fact that he was also her employer gave her an excuse to be tender to him, softening the blow. Harwood was sensitive and kind, but she wanted to make it on her own now.

If she wasn't strong enough for one, how could she ever hope to be strong enough for two?

She paused before her classroom before turning the doorknob. Dax could see the tension skimming up and down her back. Apprehension? Guilt? It was still too soon to tell.

The classroom was empty.

The children who normally occupied it had temporarily been moved to the school library until the smell of smoke could be eradicated from the room.

As if of like mind, Dax and Nathan went straight to the wastepaper basket beside the desk.

Knowing they probably preferred to have her hang back, Brenda still joined them. Even looking at the basket, burnt and misshapen, the fact that the fire had started here still amazed her. She was so careful. How could this have happened? The metal container was completely blackened, as was the side of the desk closest to the basket.

"Looks like this is the only place the fire damaged," Harwood noted.

Nathan looked around and nodded. "Lucky."

"Controlled," Dax countered. He raised his eyes to Brenda. "Whoever set this did it after the alarm went off."

Why was he looking at her like that? Did he expect her to suddenly fall to her knees and confess? "How can you tell?" Brenda asked.

He'd already made the calculations. "Because it took the firefighters less than ten minutes to get here. Ten minutes would have been enough time for the fire to have spread throughout the whole room if it had started first. The alarm was tripped and the firefighters were already on their way when the fire was set. Someone wanted to be sure that no one was hurt during all this." Dax paused as he looked at her. "Do you have any matches in the classroom?"

So much for thinking she was being paranoid. "As a matter of fact, I do."

There was no smoking allowed on the premises. Besides, he doubted if she was a smoker. There were no nicotine stains between her middle and index fingers and her teeth were blazing white. Which begged the question, "Why?"

"We have a science project going." She gestured toward the cone-shaped papier mâché structure sitting in the middle of a table in the far corner. It looked like a child's version of a tropical island. "The children and I are making a volcano."

Plausible, he thought, nodding. "Can I see the matches?"

Nerves were skittering through her as she opened the top drawer to her desk. She didn't know whether to be furious or to search for the name of a good lawyer. Reaching for the box where she kept her matches, she stopped.

"They're not here." There wasn't much to move around in the drawer, but she went through the motions with no success. "I keep them in a metal box, but it's not in here."

The taller of the two detectives said nothing, only nodded, but by now she was convinced that he thought she was involved in this more than just peripherally. Closer scrutiny into her life might only convince him of the fact. Recently widowed, her finances were not in the best of shape. Maybe he'd think that she decided to supplement it by ransoming Annie.

The very thought moved a cold shiver up and down

her spine. The nausea that she had been struggling to keep at bay threatened to overpower her.

She blew out an annoyed breath as she slammed the drawer shut harder than she'd intended. "Look, I can take a lie-detector test."

Guilty people didn't usually volunteer to do that—unless they were very, very good, Dax thought. Lie detectors were not infallible and had been known to be fooled. Still, he decided to pass—for now. "That won't be necessary."

She surprised him by not grasping at the truce he offered her. "I think it is just to get that look out of your eyes. I want you to understand that I love Annie Tyler, maybe because no one else seems to, but I think that she is a wonderful little girl who has been given a raw deal from the day she was born."

He decided to play devil's advocate just to see her reaction. "Having parents who can buy you anything you want doesn't seem like such a raw deal to me."

"Anything but their time," she pointed out evenly.

He looked at her with renewed interest. Not all kidnappings were about ransoms. Sometimes children were taken because the kidnapper thought they were rescuing the child from an unhappy life. "Maybe you could give her a better life."

"I know I could—" Brenda stopped abruptly. "I didn't take Annie. I wouldn't traumatize her like that. Besides, I was right out there in plain sight all the time," she pointed out.

That didn't constitute an ironclad alibi. "Accomplices aren't unheard of."

She'd had just about enough of this. "Detective Cavanaugh, I want a lie-detector test," she repeated. "I insist."

"We'll see what we can do to accommodate you later," Dax told her before turning toward Harwood. "Right now, I'd like to talk to some of the other teachers, see if they saw anything. And while you're at it, I'd like the address and phone number of those prospective parents Mrs. York was showing around."

"Of course," Harwood agreed quickly. "It's in my office. I'll go back and get it. Mrs. York can help you with the other teachers."

Right now, Dax thought, Mrs. York looked as if she'd rather hand his head to him on a platter.

Chapter 3

"You really suspect her?"

Nathan was leaning back against the desk at the front of the room, his attention diverted toward Brenda York. He glanced at his partner. To his left a stocky, pleasant-faced teacher was leading a gaggle of second-graders out of the art room, which had been set aside to conduct questioning.

Dax was looking at Annie Tyler's teacher from across the room. She was saying something to one of the kids who looked concerned. The boy smiled at her and nodded. She had a way about her, he thought. Made people trust her. Put them at their ease.

And at her mercy?

He glanced at his partner. "We're supposed to suspect everyone, Nathan, you know that."

Nathan gave a little shrug. His small pad inside his jacket pocket rustled against his shirt. The pages, thick with notes, were no longer smooth. "Yeah, but she seems so upset about it."

Dax smiled. "You always did have a weakness for blondes." He turned toward his partner. "The woman had access. By her own admission, she knows the little girl inside and out, that means she'd know exactly how to handle her."

Shaking his head, Nathan frowned. "What's her motive?"

She moved like poetry, Dax thought. Flowing into every step. Confident, yet incredibly feminine.

Abruptly, he wiped the thought from his mind, telling himself he had to get out more. Dax shoved his hands into his pockets. "Money's always a good motive. Most people can't have enough of it."

"So you do suspect her."

Dax shrugged. He was thinking out loud, but he and Nathan had that kind of relationship. Half-formed thoughts could be voiced in safety.

"My gut tells me no, my training tells me to hold off any final judgments."

As he watched the woman stop to comfort one of the last children in the line, Nathan sighed. "If I were single, my gut would be telling me a whole lot of other things besides hold off."

Dax laughed but made no comment. Precisely because his gut, or whatever part of him that was instrumental in allowing attraction to set in, was telling him a great deal, none of which included the phrase "hold off." If being a cop, a good cop, wasn't so ingrained in him, he might have followed through on one of any number of instincts.

As it was, he felt something stirring within him, something beyond the enormous sexual pull that kept harassing him. Harassing him because it couldn't go anywhere. She was part of a case. And she was married.

She was also human. He saw the strain on her face before she locked it away.

Leaving Nathan behind him, he crossed to her. "You looked tired. Why don't you take a break?"

The sound of the detective's voice coming from behind her startled Brenda. She'd been allowing her mind to wander for a second. And grasp onto some awful scenarios. Regaining control over her emotions, she turned around to face him.

"That won't help Annie."

The sincerity he heard in her voice crept through the layers of steeliness he'd imposed around himself whenever he was working. He had to admit she impressed him. Someone else in her position would have been looking to distance themselves from the police as they covered their own tail. But she didn't. Her concern was completely centered on the missing child.

"You know, about that lie detector test—"

Her eyes narrowed ever so slightly and she raised her chin again, as if bracing herself for a further confrontation. "Anytime, Detective."

Anytime.

If he'd had the luxury right now, he would have allowed his thoughts free rein in a fantasy. But he didn't have that luxury. What he had was a missing child.

Dax looked into her eyes. Nothing there made him doubt his decision. "I think we can skip it. The department doesn't like having its time wasted."

Was she finally allowed to get off the hook—or was he just toying with her? The thought that he suspected her of being involved in the kidnapping made her furious, never mind that logically, she knew it was his job to suspect everyone.

Brenda measured her words out slowly. "Then you finally believe that I didn't have anything to do with this?"

He knew he was stepping outside the lines, but they paid him for going with instincts, and his professional one told him exactly what Nathan's told him. That Brenda York wasn't involved in this.

His eyes held hers and something inside him fidgeted. It gave him pause. But commitment was a funny thing. Any kind of commitment, even to a state of mind. It meant boxing himself in and he didn't like to do that either. He liked the freedom that noncommitment represented.

So, he didn't answer her.

Instead, he said, "You've been a great help with the kids."

She'd had a calming effect, putting questions to them that had needed to be answered. They'd asked children from all the grades if any of them had seen anything suspicious. There'd been a few conflicting stories, none of which had amounted to anything. But even that was headway. It meant the kidnappers were very good at their job and that this had all been premeditated.

"I'm not too good with them myself," he added since the stillness made him uncomfortable.

"No children of your own?"

He knew that if his late mother had had her way, he would have been married for years by now, with half a dozen kids. Truthfully, pleasing his mother had been the only reason he'd ever considered the state of matrimony—and very nearly made a fatal mistake he would have regretted, one way or another, for the rest of his life.

Dax shook his head. "No wife of my own."

She gave him an amused look. "That doesn't answer the question."

Dax grinned. Sharp lady. "No, no kids of my own. You?"

She paused for a moment, as if about to say something, then shook her head. "No, I don't have any children." She nodded toward the last of the children filing out the door. "Those are my kids."

He had the feeling she'd almost said something else, but let it go. He was guilty of reading too much into everything. "Big family."

She moved her shoulders in a vague shrug. There

was the hint of a longing expression on her face. "I always wanted a big family."

He looked down at her left hand. Again, he wondered why there was no ring there. "How does your husband feel about that?"

The question stiffened her slightly. Everything was still raw. There hadn't been enough time for a proper scab to form over things, even though she'd never really loved Wade. Somehow, that seemed to make it all worse. He had deserved better, he'd deserved someone who could have loved him to distraction.

She looked toward the doorway, away from the detective who stirred up too many things inside of her with his questions. "My husband doesn't feel anything at all. He's dead."

Dax felt as if he'd just stomped on a delicate structure, breaking it into a hundred pieces. "Oh, I'm sorry."

In her mind's eyes, she could still see Wade, see his kind face. God, but she had tried to love him, really tried.

"Yes, so am I." She knotted her hands together before her. "Wade was a good man. He was killed in a freak accident during maneuvers." She looked at him, gauging her words, doling them out slowly only after examining them. She wasn't used to being overly cautious. She liked to be open; it was a freedom she'd embraced wholeheartedly after leaving home. But this detective put her on her guard. "He was a marine." She shifted her weight, impatient to leave the subject, impatient to get on with the pressing job of finding

Annie. "That was the last of them. Anyone else you want to question?"

He'd called in backup. Several uniformed patrolmen had searched the building from top to bottom as well as the surrounding grounds. No sign of the missing girl had turned up. No handy clues, no lost hair ribbons like in the movies. Annie Tyler didn't wear hair ribbons. And she seemed to have vanished into thin air.

In addition, the phone number the headmaster had produced as the one given by the couple Brenda had taken on the tour of the building had turned out to be bogus. No big surprise there. Dax had expected as much.

There were times he hated being right.

"No, no more questions right now. Except for you." He saw the wariness creep into her eyes. What was she waiting for him to say? "Can you describe the couple?" He looked from her to Harwood, hoping that one of them had retained enough detail to create a half-decent sketch. Most people, he knew, weren't good with details.

"I can do better than that," Brenda told him. She took a pad from the easel and picked up a newly sharpened pencil from the desk. "I can sketch them for you."

That would have been the next step, putting one or both of them together with a sketch artist. Exchanging looks with Nathan—Nathan's had unabashed admiration clearly registering in his—Dax turned back to the woman. "You can do that?"

"Drawing is my hobby," she told him. "It relaxes

me." And these days, she thought, she had to work really hard at relaxing. Decisions had to be made, events had to be faced up to.

Because her time was running out.

"Great, see what you can whip up for us." As Brenda sat down and got busy, Dax looked at Harwood. "We're going to need the little girl's address. Her parents have to be notified."

He'd held off doing that, hoping against hope to find the child without alarming her parents. He knew what his own parents had gone through the time his brother Troy had been lost in the woods while hiking with his friends. He'd been fifteen at the time and no one had taken him, but it had been harrowing nonetheless. "Missing" was one of the most pain-evoking words in the English language. It had been the worst twenty-eight hours his parents had ever gone through.

Obviously anticipating the request, Harwood produced a folded piece of paper from his pocket and surrendered it to him. On it was the Tylers' address and phone number. "Annie's father is on location in Europe. Her mother's in New York, I believe, visiting friends."

Brenda looked up from the image that was forming beneath her pencil on the sketch pad.

"I already put calls through to them," she informed Dax. "Her mother's catching the first flight out of Kennedy. Her father's taking his private jet. But neither of them will be home for several hours."

She'd jumped ahead of him again. There was no end

to the surprises this diminutive blonde delivered, Dax thought. "So if there's a ransom call—"

She'd thought of that as well. "There's a house-keeper at the house, a Martha Danridge. She's been with them for several years. I told Annie's mother it might be wise to give Ms. Danridge instructions on what she wanted her to say if the kidnappers called."

Nathan shook his head. Admiration shone in his eyes as he looked at the young woman. "You ever stop being a teacher, Mrs. York, we could certainly use you on the force."

She smiled at him, dismissing the compliment with grace. "Just covering bases."

The woman was clearheaded, Dax thought. He liked that. The women he came in contact with outside his own family tended to be a little foggy when it came to that department.

It was actually something he thought of as a plus. That way, he wouldn't be tempted to make a mistake and get involved with any of them on more than just a passing, superficial level.

He came up behind her and looked over her shoulder at the sketch she was completing. It was of the woman. Her face was gaunt and there was a slight edge to it, a sharpness that made the viewer wary. "You really can draw."

Brenda looked up at him. "I told you I could."

"So you did." He extrapolated on what she'd just told him. "You know the Tyler's housekeeper?"

"Only by sight."

She'd been to the house once, to talk to Annie's parents about Annie. Martha Danridge had let her in and brought her to Annie's mother. Annie's father was away, which seemed par for the course, and her mother, completely forgetting about the appointment that had been made to discuss Annie's painful shyness, had been on her way out. Perforce, the conversation had been brief. Rebecca Allen-Tyler had thanked her for her concern and dismissed her the way she might a waiter who'd brought the wrong order to her table.

Brenda's heart had gone out to the little girl, knowing her mother undoubtedly treated her with the same regard: as something to be suffered, but not necessarily with patience. People like that, she thought, didn't deserve having a bright, sensitive little girl like Annie.

Dax made a judgment call. "Close enough," he told her.

She didn't understand. "For what?"

He had a feeling she could smooth the way for them with the housekeeper faster than they could manage themselves. Badges tended to rattle people and the situation was already stressful enough. He'd seen her in action with both jittery teachers and anxious children. Her calming effect would be welcomed.

"I'd like you to come with us," he explained. He could feel Nathan staring at him. "You can finish the second sketch on the way there."

Brenda nodded. Her mouth curved. She was eager to do what she could. Being suddenly cast adrift while the detectives went on with the investigation would have made her insane.

"All right. I just need to stop by my room to get my things. I'll meet you outside."

Dax nodded his agreement and she hurried back to her classroom.

The stillness met her at the door the moment she opened it. It seemed to accuse her of negligence.

I'll find you, Annie, I promise I will, she vowed silently.

Taking her purse from the bottom drawer in her desk, she turned around only to swallow a gasp. Harwood was standing almost directly behind her.

"Sorry," he apologized. "I didn't mean to frighten you."

"I guess we're all a little jumpy right now." As she started for the door, he took her arm, detaining her for a moment. She looked at him quizzically.

"I just want you to know that I don't for a moment think you have anything to do with this." He paused, searching for words. She noticed that there was a thin line of perspiration on his upper lip. This had to be very difficult for him, she thought. The academy was his whole life. To have its reputation jeopardized this way had to have him cringing inwardly. "And I don't hold you responsible."

In a day and age when people were quick to shed blame and point fingers in an attempt to get attention refocused somewhere else, she was grateful for his taking the time to reassure her. He had no way of knowing about the precarious state she felt herself in.

"Thank you."

Harwood took her hand in both of his and nodded in the general direction of the front of the school. She knew he meant to indicate the two detectives who were out there, waiting for her.

"Are you up to this? Going to Annie's house, I mean. I can take you home if you're not. No one'll think the less of you."

As if she could go home. As if she could find a shred of peace until the little girl was recovered, safe and sound.

Very delicately, Brenda pulled her hand away from his. "I'm fine, Matthew," she assured him. "I just want to do anything I can to help."

He sighed and nodded. "Of course you do. We all do." He walked with her to the hall. "Call me and let me know if I can do anything for the Tylers."

"I will," she promised, then hurried down the long corridor to the massive double doors at the front of the building.

Outside, Dax and Nathan waited by the car. Unlike when they'd first arrived, there were few cars left. One by one, the teachers had all been dismissed, the children, as soon as they were quizzed, had been sent home. The only sign that something was amiss were the two patrol cars parked on the far side of the lot. But even that was being wrapped up.

Nathan waited in vain for an explanation. Finally,

he asked, "Do you know what you're doing? Isn't taking the kid's teacher along a little unorthodox? Even if she is a knockout."

"Her being a knockout has nothing to do with it and no, it's not a little unorthodox, it's a lot unorthodox," Dax corrected him. "But I've got a feeling she might be useful. She seems to know the kid pretty well and she's got this calming effect on people."

Other than himself, he added silently. One of the teachers had been close to hysteria once she discovered the reason for their presence on the premises. Brenda had calmed the woman down sufficiently so that she could give them a statement. The teacher hadn't noticed anything out of the ordinary, but if she had, Brenda would have been responsible for getting it out of her.

Besides, something told him to keep the woman close. He wasn't sure just which instincts he was going on, but by and large, he'd learned to trust them and he wasn't about to dismiss them now.

He straightened as he saw Brenda hurry through the double doors. The slight sultry breeze was playing with the ends of her hair that had come undone from the knot she'd arranged her hair into.

Damn but she was one hell of a good-looking woman, he thought again.

Martha Danridge was visibly trembling as she admitted them into what could only be termed a mansion some twenty-five minutes later. The three-storied building, complete with stables, a tennis court and two pools, sat atop a hill that was at the end of a long, winding road. The first time Brenda had seen it, she'd thought of a castle nestled in the center of a fairy tale. And Annie was the lonely princess.

Rebecca Allen-Tyler had spared the time to tell her that it was an actual castle, transplanted from Ireland and rebuilt stone by stone because she'd fallen in love with it on their honeymoon.

The king and queen, it seemed, spent hardly any time at all in their castle with their princess.

The housekeeper seemed barely capable of processing their names as Dax introduced himself and Nathan, then indicated Brenda. "And you already know Annie's teacher, Brenda York."

"Yes, I already know Mrs. York." The crisp English accent seemed at odds with the nervous expression on the older woman's face. One hand was working the edge of her apron as she closed the front door. "Mrs. Tyler isn't here."

"But she did call you," Annie said.

"Yes." Tears welled up in the woman's brown eyes and she looked close to breaking down right before them. She covered her mouth with her hands, holding back a sob until she could regain some measure of control over her voice. "How could such a terrible thing happen? That poor little bit of a thing, she must be so frightened."

Brenda slipped her arm around the woman's shoulders in mute comfort. It was the same thought that kept crossing and recrossing her own mind ever since she realized Annie wasn't out on the lawn with the rest of the class. Chillingly, she'd known that something was very, very wrong right from the first.

"The important thing is that we're going to get her back," Brenda assured the woman who sobbed into her handkerchief. The doorbell rang and Brenda's head bobbed up, alert.

"That's going to be the tech team," Dax told the housekeeper. He'd placed a call, giving them the Tylers' address, while he and Nathan had waited for Brenda.

Motioning to the housekeeper not to trouble herself, Nathan fell back and opened the front door. Two men and one woman, all carrying large black bags that looked like suitcases, walked in.

Dax approached the housekeeper. "We're going to need to place bugs on all your phone lines."

"Yes, of course," Martha whispered, her voice cracking.

She was still shaking, Brenda noted. Again she slipped her arm around the woman's thin shoulders and gave her a little squeeze.

"Why don't you show them where all the phones are?" she suggested gently.

Like a marionette whose string had been pulled, Martha nodded, her head bobbing up and down.

But before she could leave the foyer, Dax moved in front of her. "There hasn't been a ransom call yet, has there?"

"No." She swallowed hard, renewed panic entering her eyes as she looked from one detective to the other, and then at Brenda. "At least, I don't think so. I was out at the store until just a little while ago, when Mrs. Tyler called me. There are no messages on the answering machine," she tagged on as if to cover her absence.

Dax didn't know if the woman was simpleminded or just addled by the situation. "Kidnappers don't generally leave messages on answering machines."

"Oh." She seemed completely deflated as she looked to Brenda for help.

"You have caller ID, don't you?" Brenda asked. It seemed a safe enough assumption. A power couple like Annie's parents would want the service to help them avoid people they didn't want to talk to.

Again, Martha bobbed her head up and down. Brenda saw a phone in the living room and crossed to it. She spun the dial located in the upper right-hand corner. No calls other than the one with a 212 area code had registered in the last three hours. That would have been Annie's mother, calling from New York with instructions for the housekeeper.

Brenda looked at Dax and shook her head. He turned toward the team Nathan had just admitted. "Let's get those taps set up. The kidnappers might be calling any minute now."

No sooner were the words out of his mouth than the telephone began to ring.

Everyone froze.

Chapter 4

Martha stared at the pristine white telephone as if it were a giant snake, coiled and poised to spring at her. Her eyes were huge as she turned them on Dax.

"Oh, my God, it's ringing." Fear resonated in her voice. "What do I do?"

It was too late to set up the wire tap. They had to hope for a second call. Dax looked at the housekeeper. "Answer it," he ordered

She began to visibly tremble.

"I can't," the housekeeper choked out the words. "Please don't make me." Frantic, Martha looked from one detective to the other. "What if I say the wrong thing? I just couldn't live with myself if something happens to that child because of me—"

Dax did a poor job of hiding his exasperation. The

seconds were ticking away fast and the phone continued to ring. "Look, lady—"

Not knowing what else to do, afraid that the moment and the call would slip through their fingers, Brenda snatched up the receiver.

"Tyler residence," she enunciated in what she prayed was a fair imitation of Martha's English accent.

Surprised, Dax stared at her. In desperation, because the kidnapper might be expecting a woman's voice on the other end, he was about to tell Brenda to answer the telephone, but she'd anticipated him. The woman had a cool head, he thought.

Making eye contact, he indicated that she should keep the person on the other end of the line talking. If the kidnapper talked, there was a slim chance that a clue, a noise in the background, might be picked up, one that would help them locate where Annie Tyler was being held.

Brenda felt as if her stomach was going to revolt and come surging out of her mouth any time now. Her morning communes with the porcelain bowl were a thing of the past only by two weeks. And this felt much worse than morning sickness.

Concentrating on the kidnapper, she was still vaguely aware that six sets of eyes were trained on her.

The police technicians and two detectives were gathered in a semicircle around her, obviously straining to hear the other side of the conversation. She held on to the receiver with both hands, tilting the ear piece slightly so that at least some of the dialogue could be made out. Out of the corner of her eye, she saw Martha sinking onto the sofa.

The instant she heard the voice on the other end, Brenda knew she hadn't a prayer of trying to recognize it. The kidnapper could have been a man or a woman for all she knew. They were using a voice synthesizer. The irritating vibrations sounded like words being blown through a harmonica.

"We have the little girl. We don't want to harm her."

You bastards. Brenda struggled to keep her feelings from spilling out. "And we do not want her harmed," she told the caller, plucking words out of nowhere. Her mind felt as if it was completely blank. "What do you want us to do?"

The voice on the other end of the line paused, as if playing out the moment. Brenda could feel the tension rising with every second that passed. "Tell the Tylers we want two million dollars and then she'll be returned. That shouldn't be hard for them to manage."

Dax suddenly grabbed Nathan's jacket and pulled it open. His partner jumped, staring at him accusingly. "Hey."

The protest faded as Dax took out his pad and the pen he kept there and began to quickly scribble something down. Done, he held the pad up for her to read as the metallic voice droned in her ear.

She squinted, trying to make out the words he'd written. The detective had alternated between printing and using script, both of which were almost illegible. Giving him an exasperated look, she filled in the gaps as best as she could.

"How do we know she's still alive?" Brenda asked. She kept her eyes on Dax. "We want proof." Dax nodded as she got his message right. "A photograph of Annie holding today's newspaper in her hands."

This time, there was no pause. There was anger. "We're the ones with all the cards here, bitch. We make the terms, not you."

She suppressed the urge to beg the kidnapper not to hurt Annie, to let her go. That would only empower him or her. Instead, she reiterated more forcefully, "We need proof."

When there was no answer, she raised her eyes to Dax for instruction. To her horror, he took hold of her wrist and pushed her hand down until the receiver was back in its cradle.

He'd made her hang up the phone.

She stared at him, stunned and furious. "What the hell are you doing?"

"The kidnapper was going to hang up on you."

She couldn't believe what he was saying. "So I got him first, is that it?" she demanded heatedly.

There was an edge to his voice. Because the risk wasn't foolproof. But rules needed to be established. "He's right, he's got all the cards. But if he feels that way, we stand less of a chance of getting the girl back, even if we do hand over the money."

"If?" she echoed. "We're not going to do what they say? This isn't a statistic, Detective, this is a little girl we're talking about. A living, breathing, please God, little girl. We have to do what they say." Her eyes narrowed accusingly as she looked at him and then toward the telephone. "Provided, of course, that they call back."

"They'll call back," he said with a conviction he didn't quite feel. The others said nothing to contradict him, but he knew that Nathan didn't approve of what he'd done.

Dax sweated out the next minute and a half as they dragged themselves up, a microsecond at a time.

The phone rang again.

Though she'd been waiting for it, praying for it, the sound made her jump. Relief flooding through her, her knees feeling almost too weak to support her, Brenda jerked the receiver up and placed it to her ear.

"Hello?"

She was aware of Dax peeling the earpiece back from her ear so that he could hear. Brenda resisted the urge to hold it in place.

"Don't you ever, ever do that to me again, bitch!" There was barely suppressed fury in the kidnapper's voice. "Or you get to hear the bullet go through her head. Understood?"

She couldn't even swallow. There was no saliva left in her mouth. "Understood."

Again there was a pause. She could feel the moments pulsating.

"You'll have your picture," the clipped, metallic

voice finally told her. "I'll call back tomorrow and tell you where you can find it."

"Tomorrow?" Brenda thought of Annie having to endure the night as a prisoner somewhere. Annie, frightened, thinking no one would come for her. That nobody cared. "Why not today?"

"Because I said so."

The line went dead.

"Hello? Hello?" Helpless, she looked up at Dax. "He hung up."

Very gently, Dax took the receiver out of her hand and replaced it in its cradle. "You did great," he told her. The woman looked as if she was going to sag to the floor right in front of him. He put his arm around her shoulders, offering her support. She seemed to stiffen against him. "You want to sit down?"

Brenda deliberately shrugged him off. "No. What I want is to find Annie."

"Yeah, we all do." Battling to keep frustration at bay, he scrubbed his hand over his face, then looked at her. He'd heard everything she had, but she'd been a microinch closer to the receiver. Maybe that was enough. "Did you hear anything in the background, anything at all?"

She shook her head. "It was like talking to ET's evil twin. I couldn't even tell you if it was a man or woman. But 'he' kept switching his pronouns, interchanging 'I' and 'we' several times. That means there's at least two of them."

He nodded. It just reinforced his suspicions that

the bogus couple who'd asked for a tour of the school were the ones who had taken the little girl. It would have helped if Harwood Academy had surveillance cameras in place, but for a prestigious school, they were appallingly lax in electronic security. A condition he figured the headmaster was going to fix—if he was given a chance. He suspected the kidnapping was going to cost the man some withdrawals.

He looked at Brenda. Unlike the housekeeper, she'd kept her cool throughout the ordeal. He knew it couldn't have been easy on her. "Quick thinking on your part, using that accent."

"I thought they might know the Tylers had an English housekeeper." She realized the admission underscored the fact that she subconsciously agreed with the detective. Someone had gone through a great deal of trouble to plot this all out. Her eyes lit as information worked its way forward through her brain. The kidnapper hadn't demanded to speak to either parent. "The kidnapper seemed to know that neither of Annie's parents were home."

Dax nodded. "They did their homework. This wasn't a random snatch, this was very well planned."

The thought chilled her. Had she been observed as well? In the classroom, had someone been watching? For how long? The north side of her classroom was completely exposed with a large bay window that comprised half the wall. She pushed the thought away.

She saw Nathan retrieve his notepad and then place it back into his pocket. "You know," she told Dax, "you've got pretty lousy handwriting. You should do something about that."

It was nothing he hadn't heard before. His sister Janelle had said his notes all looked as if they'd been done by a drunken spider whose legs had been dipped in ink. "You managed to read it, didn't you?"

She laughed shortly. "Only because I'm versed in scribble."

"Whatever it takes," he responded. Dax turned his attention to the housekeeper. Seeing him look at her, the woman tried to rally but rising from the sofa seemed to be more than she could manage at the moment. He crouched before her. "Have you noticed any strangers around here lately?"

Martha didn't have to pause to reflect. "Mrs. Tyler's having the guest house remodeled."

That meant that any number of people could be on the premises without having to justify themselves. Anyone could have passed himself off as a plumber, an electrician, a plasterer.

Dax shook his head. "Plenty of opportunity for people to be coming and going." He looked at Brenda. "Where are the sketches you made?"

She'd finished the second one on the way over. "In the car."

He turned toward Nathan. Nothing more had to be said. "I'm on it," Nathan told him, leaving.

"No, I can't be sure." Martha shook her head as she looked from one sketch to the other that Dax held before her. Her eyes returned to the one of the man. "Him, maybe, but…" Her voice trailed off as she looked up at Dax helplessly. "They do tend to blend in together. Mrs. Tyler is always having something remodeled."

"Yeah, I got that problem, too," Nathan muttered, gathering the two sketches together.

They were striking out when they should be forging forward. Brenda turned toward Dax. "Now what?"

Her eyes were bright, he thought, as if she was barely harnessing the energy within her. He knew what she had to be feeling. Desire to do something was knotted up with the realization that everything was moving forward much too slowly.

"Now some of the patrolmen and I get a canvas of the area around the school grounds, see if anyone might have noticed something." He glanced at his partner. "Nathan, see if we can get those sketches onto the local news stations—"

At the suggestion, the housekeeper came to life. She rose to her feet, her expression utterly horrified. "Mr. Tyler wouldn't want the media alerted. He absolutely abhors publicity about his personal life."

While he was sensitive to a parent's anguish, Dax could have cared less what an overpaid Hollywood director did or didn't want.

"I'm afraid this is out of Mr. Tyler's hands," Dax told the woman crisply, then because she still looked terrified, he relented. "The public is incredibly helpful, Ms. Danridge. Someone might have seen something."

And that, he thought, was all the time he had to spare for hand-holding. He turned to his partner. "Nathan, we're going to need phone lines set up at the precinct for the calls that are going to start coming in."

The notepad was out again. "You pulling together a task force?"

"That's what I'm doing," Dax responded glibly.

He looked as if he was about to walk out. Brenda shifted so that she was directly in his path. "What can I do?"

Dax would have thought that by now, all she would have wanted to do was go home. "You've already done a great deal."

He was putting her off, she could tell by the tone of his voice. She didn't want to be swept under the rug. "What can I do?" she repeated.

He glanced over toward the technician who was wiring the telephone Brenda had just used in hope that when the kidnapper called the next time, they might be able to trace the call. Even if they did, he had a hunch it would probably be coming from a public phone. But sometimes they got lucky.

The blonde with the killer legs was still waiting for him to answer her. "You could stay here and talk to the Tylers when they arrive home." He was leaving someone from the task force to speak to them, but there was no harm in their seeing a familiar face, especially if that familiar face could walk them through what had happened at the school.

He was brushing her off. "Mrs. Tyler won't be due

in for another couple of hours and Mr. Tyler will probably be here in the morning."

"Good estimate." Sidestepping her, he set his sights on the front door.

Didn't he understand that she could be useful? That she knew Annie better than anyone and that maybe that knowledge might be helpful? Moving quickly, she got in his way again. "What do I do until then?"

He put his hands on her shoulders and deliberately moved her to the side, out of his way. "You might try praying," he told her as he left.

She was at her wits' end.

The journey to that destination hadn't been an overly long one. As the brash, annoying Detective Cavanaugh had suggested, she'd remained at the Tyler estate, waiting for Annie's mother to arrive. Secretly, she'd hoped that perhaps the kidnapper might have a change of heart and call again.

But he didn't.

Trying to keep her frustration under wraps, she'd spent the time she was waiting for Rebecca Allen-Tyler to make her appearance talking to the policeman who had been left on duty.

Exactly seven hours after she had placed the call to her, Annie's mother swept into the mansion riding on a tide of reporters. By now, the story of Annie's kidnapping as well as her sketches of the two kidnappers had led off every station's evening news broadcast.

The little girl's abduction from the Harwood Academy was fodder for the newest media feeding frenzy.

Brenda braced herself as she faced the former actress. To her credit, Annie's mother did look distraught, and she did have the housekeeper shut out the media reporters. Her personal bodyguard, a man who looked as if he'd just walked off with the Mr. Olympia bodybuilding crown, stood like a towering sentry at the front entrance.

"How could you have allowed something like this happen?" Rebecca screamed at her the moment she recognized her.

"Mrs. Tyler, I'm very, very sorry—" Brenda began.

"Sorry? You don't know the meaning of the word sorry. You'll be sorry all right, sorry you were ever born when Simon and I finish suing your asses off for this."

She'd already given the woman the details over the telephone when she'd placed the original call. Brenda supposed that three thousand miles was a long distance to work up her anger. That didn't excuse what had come out of the woman's mouth, though.

"With all due respect, Mrs. Tyler, we thought there was a fire going on. And if it were my daughter, my first thoughts wouldn't be about suing people, it would be about moving heaven and earth to get her back."

"How dare you!" Rebecca Tyler shrieked. "How dare you?"

Brenda looked at the patrolman closest to her. "I

don't think I'm needed here right now." She began to leave.

The patrolman came to life. "Wait, Detective Cavanaugh said I was to take you to your car."

Her car was still parked in the school lot. She was about to call for a cab, but this made things easier. "Always thinking, your detective."

The patrolman flashed her a smile. "We like to think so."

Once they got past the media reporters camped outside the door, the trip was relatively quick. Hers was the only vehicle left in the lot. Danvers, the patrolman, pulled up beside it.

Dusk had descended, and with it a strange clamminess in the air. It was a strange May night. But then, it had been a strange day all around.

"I can follow you home," Danvers offered as she unlocked her car.

She shook her head. "I'll be fine," she assured him. Brenda got into the driver's seat. She thought of the scene they'd just left behind. "I think your partner might need help with Mrs. Tyler, though. You'd better get back there."

Danvers sighed, looking none too happy. "Right."

As he drove off, she turned her key in the ignition. But as she began to drive out of the lot, she changed her mind. Making a U-turn that brought her right back to where she'd parked, she turned off the engine.

The night promised to be a very long one. She sincerely doubted she was going to get any sleep. If she was going to remain awake, she might as well put the time to good use.

She needed to feel as if she was doing something. Anything.

Getting out of her car, she locked it again, then walked slowly toward the school. The evening was eerily quiet. The sound of her heels hitting the concrete reverberated back to her, adding to the surreal atmosphere.

There was yellow police tape draped across the front entrance. She debated ducking under it, then decided to use the side door.

The way the kidnapper probably had, she reasoned. Except that Brenda had a key.

"Hang on, Annie," she whispered to the night air. "We'll have you home soon."

She refused to believe anything else.

"What are you doing here?"

Brenda shrieked as she spun around. She nearly jumped out of her chair and wound up hitting her knee against the side of the desk. Nerves vibrated throughout her entire body as she pressed a hand to her hammering heart. Her throbbing knee would have to wait.

As far as she'd known, the building was empty.

She stared at Dax in the doorway.

"That's some scream you have there," Dax commented as he approached her. He nodded toward her leg. "Your knee okay?"

It throbbed, and there would probably be a bruise,

but that was of no consequence. She shrugged carelessly.

"I'll be fine." As soon as my heart stops pounding. It didn't seem to be an appropriate comment to share with the good-looking detective at the moment.

What was she doing here, he wondered. Was she more deeply involved than he'd thought? "There's yellow tape on the outside of the doors," he pointed out.

"Yes, I know."

He noticed the tape hadn't been touched. She'd probably used the side entrance. "That means it's a crime scene."

She knew that, too. But this was the only place she could think of that had the proper tools she needed in order to work up the flyers with Annie's picture.

Sitting at the state-of-the-art-computer, she indicated the printer. There was a stack of colored flyers beside it. "I wanted to print up flyers to distribute around the area. The school has the best program for that sort of thing."

"You have a photograph of Annie?"

"I always take photographs of my class during the school year. I like to keep albums."

She didn't add that having photographs of the various children and tracing their progress over the school year helped to give her the sense of family she so sorely lacked in her own life.

Dax picked up one of the flyers she'd run off from the industrial-sized printer. It looked very professional. "I'm impressed."

She thought he was referring to the equipment. "Mr. Harwood feels that the students deserve nothing but the best at the school."

"No, I meant by the flyer." He put it back on top of the pile. "Nice work."

She shrugged. "It's not hard when you know how."

He wouldn't have thought that a woman who looked the way she did would be so self-deprecating. Every time he gave her a compliment, she discounted it.

Having replenished the paper just before he'd entered the room, Brenda pressed the print button again. "What are you doing here?"

"I was driving by, I saw the light." In actuality, he'd come by to see if she'd picked up her car yet. Seeing a light in the second-story window had made him investigate.

She tried to second-guess his reasoning. "And thought the kidnappers might have come back to the scene of the crime?"

"Actually," he leaned against the desk, looking down at her, "I didn't know what to think." And that, he decided, was the case here with her. Every time he made up his mind about Brenda York, something else was thrown into the mix. "I try not to jump to conclusions until all the evidence is in." And then, because the moment was so serious and begged to be lightened, he smiled at her. "But it doesn't hurt to stay on top of things."

The air felt a little rare. She moved back a little. "How did the canvas turn out?"

"Nothing so far." How long did it take for perfume to fade, he wondered. Hers was still getting to him. He rose, moving back toward the printer. "We have an Amber Alert going." Over the last couple of years, it had become standard procedure every time a child went missing. Descriptions of the little girl now flashed across freeway signs up and down the state. A great deal of distance could be covered in eight hours.

She nodded toward the radio she had on beside the desk. "Yes, I know."

She'd been on his mind ever since he'd left her at the Tyler estate. He wasn't even sure exactly why, but she was, lingering in the corners like the scent of some potent flower drifting invisibly through the warm summer night air. When he'd gone back to the Tylers— and spent some time with a tearful Mrs. Tyler—Danvers had told him he'd dropped her off at the school.

Seeing her car in the lot had given him a measure of concern. And made him wonder if he'd written her off a little too soon.

"How are you doing?"

She blew out a breath. Maybe it was because she was too tired, or too stressed, but for once in her life, she didn't hide her feelings behind a smoke screen. "Not too well."

Chapter 5

Looking closer at her, he could see the definite signs of weariness. Her skin was almost translucent.

He curbed the urge to run the back of his knuckles against her cheek, as if that could somehow bring the color back to her face.

The girl's abduction had taken a toll on her. He thought of his gut feelings, the instincts that had absolved Brenda of the crime. If she was faking it, then she was a damn better actress than he would have thought she was.

"How did it go with Mrs. Tyler?"

"Not well." She was trying to be charitable toward the other woman, but it was difficult. Frowning as she remembered the encounter at the mansion, Brenda pushed herself away from the desk. "She blames the school, blames me." She sighed, dragging her hand through her hair. "Is probably on the phone with her lawyer right now, discussing a lawsuit."

He parked himself on the corner of the desk. He'd formed his own opinions about the actress after only several minutes in her presence. His sympathies were entirely on Brenda's side.

"Lawsuit?"

Brenda nodded. "Those were the last words Rebecca Allen-Tyler said to me. That she was going to 'sue my ass.'"

Was that what had drained the color from Brenda's face? Fear of being taken to court? "I don't think you really have to worry about that."

The threat had never concerned her. She had precious little that could be taken from her.

"I'm not worried. I'm annoyed, maybe, but not worried." Her thoughts returned to Annie. "Not about her, anyway."

"Annoyed?" He wasn't sure he followed her. "Why annoyed?"

Try as she might to suppress it, her anger rose up like bile in her throat. She thought of the sad look in Annie's eyes when she tried to get the little girl to talk about her mother.

"Because this woman can't spare fifteen minutes for that little girl. Because she's always 'on,' not to mention the fact that she's usually away on some trip. And now suddenly she wants to sue everybody because her daughter's been kidnapped? Why isn't her first concern to do everything she can to have Annie found? Why isn't she taking herself to task because up until now, she's been such a lousy mother?" With every word, her anger grew. "I went to see her once to discuss Annie's shyness with her and she fluffed me off—this after breaking I don't know how many appointments." She struggled to calm herself down. "Rebecca Allen-Tyler is not my candidate for mother of the year."

"What about her father?" When he'd left the house, Simon Tyler hadn't returned yet.

Brenda waved her hand in dismissal. "Worse than her mother." It struck her as such a tragedy. And it all could have been avoided. "Annie worships the ground they both walk on and they just keep walking on it, not bothering to look down, not seeing the wonderful little human being they're ignoring."

He couldn't help notice that the color had returned to her cheeks. And that it made her even more attractive. "You sound pretty passionate about this."

She blew out a breath as she sighed. "Maybe because I am. I hate seeing a kid get a raw deal." The printer had stopped. She hit the appropriate button again. The machine began spitting out fresh flyers. "They've got such a very short time to be innocent, they should be allowed to enjoy it."

"Did you?"

Brenda raised her head, caught off guard by the question. "What?"

"Did you?" he repeated. When she continued to

look at him quizzically, he elaborated on the reason for his question. "I get the feeling you're speaking from firsthand experience." In response, she got up and crossed to the printer, her back to him. He'd struck a nerve, he thought. "What was your childhood like?"

She lifted her shoulder in a vague, noncommittal shrug. She'd talked too much. That was her problem, she thought. She always shared herself too quickly. You would have thought that she would have learned not to by now. That having a mother who abandoned her and a father who took out every failure in his life on her would have taught her to keep her own council. Even Wade had been closemouthed and had cut her off more than once when she tried to talk to him, to get him to share his feelings with her.

All of her life, there had been nothing but emotional disappointment after emotional disappointment. Except for the children.

"I don't remember," she murmured, putting more paper into the printer's tray. "It was a long time ago."

She was putting him off. But he had a feeling she needed to talk, so he pressed. "Not that long ago, you're what, twenty-two?"

"Twenty-six."

Because she continued to keep her back to him, Dax rounded the printer and faced her. "I'm impressed, you preserve well."

She laughed then and it was like the breeze weaving its way through wind chimes. Not the annoying ones like his neighbor had that clanged, but the small ones, the ones that sounded like music.

"That's nice," he told her softly. "You should do that more often."

She stopped stacking the finished flyers beside the printer. "Do what?"

"Laugh."

Her thoughts returned to Annie. "I guess there isn't that much to laugh about right now."

He curbed the urge to put his hand on her shoulder, to make some sort of contact that could convey comfort far better than any words that might come out of his mouth. "There will be. We'll find her."

Her mouth curved slightly. Sadly. She wished she could believe him. But she knew what the world was like. "You sound so certain."

"Only way to go."

She looked at him for a long moment, gazed into his eyes. He truly believed that, she realized. It gave her a measure of comfort to have the man in charge of the investigation so sure of the results. She wouldn't have thought that a cop could be this optimistic.

"You must have had a very good childhood."

"As a matter of fact, I did."

With little effort, she could almost see him as a child. Bright, gregarious, taking over any room he walked into. "Apple of your mother's eye?"

More like the source of most of her gray hair. "I don't know about that. There were too many of us around to be anyone's favorite."

Because she was one, she'd pictured him as an only child. "How many is too many?"

Dax paused, doing a head count. "Eleven, counting me."

Brenda was aware that her mouth had dropped open. "Your mother had eleven children?" At least she got a chance to go home at night. Being responsible for that many little souls twenty-four hours a day seemed like the surest path to early burnout to her. "That poor woman. She probably didn't have time to even eat an apple, much less—"

Dax held up his hand, laughing. "No, after four kids Mom told Dad that if he wanted any more, he was going to find a way to push them out himself because she wasn't going to have to go through morning sickness again."

Morning sickness.

God, could she certainly identify with that, Brenda thought. But at least his mother had had his father to lean on. Someone who was there, who wanted to have children with her. She and Wade had never really discussed having children, something else he kept putting off talking about. She'd discovered that she was pregnant and that Wade had been accidentally killed during maneuvers all in the same day.

Getting pregnant had been an accident as well. She and Wade had been separated for almost four months when he'd come to her, asking her if she'd be willing to try to make a go of their marriage again. She'd felt so guilty over marrying him in the first place just to get away from home that she felt she owed it to him. So she had said yes.

Wade put in for a three-day pass and they went down to San Diego. They'd stayed at a little bed and breakfast inn just off the beach. She could hear the seagulls calling to one another.

The long weekend had gone by without anything being resolved. Wade went back to his world and she to hers, their future still up in the air.

She'd been sick almost from the start, but had been afraid to take a pregnancy test, afraid to put her suspicions into words. She fervently prayed that if she ignored it, somehow, it would all go away.

But it hadn't, and there was life growing inside of her now. A life that she vowed to love and protect the way she had never been herself. The way she hadn't for Annie.

She looked at Dax. "Then where did the eleven come from?"

"Cousins as well as siblings."

He took it for granted that everyone knew. It was such a way of life, such a given for him that at times he forgot that not everyone was aware of the fact that he had cousins and brothers who liberally populated various departments within the Aurora police force. That his Uncle Andrew had once been the police chief of the city before he retired and that his father, Brian, was now the current chief of detectives.

He grinned. "I've got tons of cousins."

Cousins. A big family, all there for one another if

she was interpreting his expression correctly. "And you're all close."

He heard the wistful note in her voice. "Sometimes too close," he told her. "There's always someone looking over your shoulder."

"Always someone looking out for you," she countered. When he didn't try to correct her, she knew she was right. What would that have been like, to have someone to turn to when things got tough? "You have no idea how lucky you are."

His grin widened. "If I forget, there's always someone around to tell me." When he was a kid, he saw a downside to that. "And I never got to get away with anything. There was always someone who saw or found out about it and word would always get back to my parents."

She heard the affection in his voice. She would have given anything to have had his life. "You're close to them, too? Your parents?"

He thought of his father. Other than a few years of typical teenager rebellion, he'd always been able to talk to the man. Like the old joke went, the older he got, the smarter his father became.

"Yeah, I guess. To my dad. My mom died a little over five years ago."

"Oh, I'm sorry. But at least you had her for a long time."

There was something in her tone that told him they had this in common. "When did your mother die?"

Brenda looked up at him, debating changing the

subject. But he had allowed her a peek into his life; it seemed rude somehow to abruptly terminate the conversation. Besides, it had all happened such a long time ago. She was beyond hurting now, she told herself. Or so she liked to believe.

"She didn't. She left."

Things began to fall into place. That was why Brenda was so passionate about Rebecca Allen-Tyler's lack of maternal love. Because she identified with the kidnapped little girl.

He thought of his Uncle Andrew. Aunt Rose had walked out after an argument and had gone missing for fifteen years. In her case, there'd been an accident with the car and they had all thought she was dead. Everyone except for his uncle. And, as it turned out, everyone except for his uncle had been wrong. Aunt Rose had been a victim of amnesia.

"Just like that?" he prodded.

She reflected. "No, not just like that. It was probably a long time in coming. My father wasn't exactly the easiest man to live with. She finally couldn't take it anymore. Neither could I, but I was too young to pack up and go." She saw the question in his eyes. "I was nine at the time."

"A lot of kids run away at nine. Younger." He'd seen the files to prove it.

He had a point, she supposed. There were times when she sat in the dark in her room after a particularly bad confrontation with her father, sobbing. Wanting desperately to find a way out of her life. But there had been no one to turn to.

She gathered the flyers together, placing them on top of the others.

"Maybe I thought things out too much. I didn't like the idea of living on the street. Besides, I kept hoping that one day my father would wake up and have an epiphany—" It all seemed so silly now. She should have known better, even then. "That he'd realize that I was one hell of a little girl and that he should appreciate all that love I had to give him."

Dax felt something protective stir within him, even though the events had taken place in the past and there was nothing he could do about them now. It still didn't change the fact that he wanted to hold her to him, to comfort her. "But he didn't."

She blew out a breath. "No, he didn't." She turned and looked at him. How had all that come out? She'd shared more with him in this short space of time than she ever could with Wade. "So, how much do you charge by the hour, doctor?"

He smiled and shook his head. "The first hundred hours are free. Call it my cousin-training."

"They all come to you with their problems?" He didn't strike her as the counseling type. Yet here she was, running off at the mouth around him, she reminded herself.

Dax felt he had no particular claim to that position. "We all come to each other whenever the occasion calls for it. I guess it's a little like having your own support group," he decided.

He'd never really thought of it that way before, but it was true. None of them had ever felt alone, not even his cousin Patrick, he guessed, and Patrick was the one who along with his sister, Patience, had had a troubled childhood. Uncle Mike, he'd discovered after piecing things together he'd overheard and had been told by his cousin Shaw, had been the insecure brother. Sandwiched in between Andrew and Brian, Mike always felt as if they outshone him with their achievements. Early on it had frustrated him and he'd taken it out on his family, drinking too much, being verbally abusive, finding solace with other women.

Dax knew that both his father and his Uncle Andrew, especially his uncle, had tried very hard to smooth things over for Patrick and Patience, to give them as secure a feeling of home and hearth as they could. Patience was the optimistic one, she was easy. But Patrick had presented a challenge when he was growing up.

Things had eventually turned out all right and now Patrick was married and expecting his first little Cavanaugh.

Yes, Dax thought, he was lucky. They all were. A simple roll of the dice and fate could have given him the life of the woman next to him.

And yet, Brenda seemed unscathed by it. Sharp, dedicated and passionate.

It was the passion that was arousing him now, he

realized. Passion in anyone always made them appear more alive, more vivid. In a woman as beautiful as Brenda York, it was especially alluring.

He rose to join her. "So, is there anyone special in your life right now?"

Brenda nodded. He felt a sinking feeling in the pit of his stomach, as if he'd lost something. But that was ridiculous, he told himself, because he hadn't had anything to begin with.

"A classroom full of special someones," she told him.

Somewhere deep inside of him, a ray of hope nudged its way forward. "You're talking about the kids in your class."

She smiled and for the first time, he saw a light enter her eyes. The sexual pull he felt was almost overwhelming.

"Yes."

"I was talking about someone taller." Initially, when he'd come to the school, she and Harwood had seemed rather tight. "The headmaster—"

Her eyes widened at the suggestion. "Matthew? No. Oh God, no. He's just a very kind man."

He'd picked up something in the headmaster's manner toward her. It had made him wonder if they'd had a prior or present relationship. "Looked as if he'd like to be kinder if you let him."

Was it that evident? She felt protective of the man who had given her a job when others wouldn't. She'd been more than a few credits short of her teaching credentials when she'd come to Harwood Academy. He'd allowed her to teach while working on her degree.

"Maybe, but I don't have that kind of relationship with him. That would be mixing business with my private life."

"And you like the lines to stay clear." It wasn't a guess. He could tell by the way she spoke.

"It keeps things simpler."

What he was feeling right now wasn't simple. It was very, very complicated. Although he liked women in all sizes and shapes and had a social life that would have contented any two normal men, he'd always been careful not to step over a line, not to mix his professional and private life.

But right now, he was entertaining thoughts that definitely crossed all the lines.

"It's getting late." He nodded toward the printer. It had stopped humming several minutes ago. "Have you finished doing what you came to do?"

By her count, she'd printed up a thousand flyers. She took two boxes that the initial paper had been packaged in and deposited the eight- by ten-inch sheets into them. It was a start. "Yes, for now."

"Good." Stacking one box on top of another, Dax picked them both up. "I'll walk you to your car," he told her.

The entire time he'd spent with her at the school, she couldn't shake the feeling that she was keeping him from something. Maybe he'd driven up here for a reason other than the one he'd given her.

"You don't have to."

He was already standing in the doorway, waiting for her to join him. "I don't have anything pressing to do at the moment."

Closing down the computer and switching off the printer, she picked up her purse and then joined him. "You're just afraid I'm going to stay here."

"Maybe," he allowed.

Waiting for her to cross the threshold, he shut the light off.

The night was warm and musky, one of those spring evenings that acted as a preview to the summer that was barely waiting in the wings. The dusk that had been there when she arrived had given way to a velvety night.

The full moon shone on the lot, casting a pool of light on the asphalt. It illuminated their way far better than the two street lamps located at the far end of the sidewalk.

Like two strangers seeking company, his car was parked beside hers. Dax watched her open the passenger door. She indicated that he should place the two boxes of flyers on the seat.

He set them down on the passenger seat. "You didn't lock the door," he admonished.

"I forgot." She didn't tell him that she often left it unlocked. It was easier that way. And maybe she was too trusting for her own good. "It's an old car, I didn't think anyone would think it worth stealing."

Brenda closed the door, then walked around to the driver's side. She turned to face him. She could feel the heat from his body even though he gave her a little space. Her hormones, she thought, were giving her a hard time. The warm night didn't help things either.

She raised the hair from the back of her neck, wishing for a breeze. Her silent entreaty went unanswered. "Well, thank you for not busting me."

Busy memorizing the gentle slope of her neck, he didn't follow her meaning. "For what?"

"For disregarding the yellow tape and going into the school."

He grinned, vainly trying to summon up cold thoughts. "Don't make a habit of it."

"I won't, I promise." Opening the driver's side door, she hesitated.

"What?"

Brenda bit her lip, then forged ahead. "The kidnapper said he'd call tomorrow. I should be there to talk to him."

He knew what she was thinking. That since she'd pretended to be the housekeeper, she should be there just in case. But that had been just because neither of the Tylers had been there to take the call. That had since changed.

"Mrs. Tyler is probably going to want to handle that," he pointed out.

He was right, of course, but she still wanted to be there, even though she knew she wasn't exactly welcome. The thought of being excluded, of being on the outside and not knowing what was happening, was painful to her. "Right. I just—"

"Want to be there," he supplied. It wasn't difficult to guess what was on her mind.

"Yes."

He looked at the boxes of flyers on the seat. "You could always bring those by tomorrow. That'll get your foot in the door."

She could see Mrs. Tyler taking them from her then closing the door on her face. "But what do I do after that?"

"Maybe we'll get lucky and the kidnapper'll call while you're there."

"And if he doesn't?"

He glanced down at her foot, then smiled. "I'll see what I can do to keep the rest of you in after that."

Gratitude shone in her eyes. The pull he'd been battling against increased, doubling. "Thank you."

"My pleasure."

And then, before he knew what he was doing, before he had a chance to tell himself not to, before he could blame it on the warm night and hours that were too long to allow him to think clearly, Dax framed her incredibly beautiful face in his hands.

Her eyes met his.

His resolve, what there was left of it, slipped away into the night.

He brought his mouth down to hers.

Chapter 6

He'd caught her by surprise.

But surprise faded quickly. In its place came the realization that she'd actually been anticipating this all along. On some plane, she'd known this was going to happen, been waiting for it to happen. In a way, she'd been holding her breath until it did.

In the space of a very quick heartbeat, Brenda wound her arms around his neck and leaned her body into his, losing herself in the taste of his lips, in the heat of his kiss.

Feeling so desperately alone these days, weighed down by the secret she was harboring, she needed this warmth, this human contact, if only for a moment. She found it comforting—and wildly exhilarating. Every part of her body was wide awake, alert, and quickly absorbing the sensations that were traveling through her body with the speed of lightning bolts.

Her eyes closed, her head spinning, Brenda moaned as the kiss deepened, pulling her in by virtue of its sheer power.

The sound of her moan echoed in his head, fueling the desire that had suddenly broken free of its shackles. He'd surprised himself by stepping outside the lines and giving in to the ever-increasing demand he'd felt drumming through his body. Dax was surprised too by the power with which his action had been met. He hadn't known what to expect, either from her response or from her. She could have slapped him, but she didn't. Could have been impassive, but she wasn't.

And she hadn't just surrendered, she'd advanced an offensive of her own and left him utterly caught up in what was happening. Turning him into a prisoner as well as an instigator.

She felt warm and supple against him, her curves yielding, making him want what he couldn't have. What the hell was going on here? What was he doing? his mind demanded sharply.

Stepping back while he still had the wherewithal, Dax looked at the woman who was now in his arms. His mind scrambled erratically in different directions, searching for a way to form an apology.

Words felt like cardboard in his mouth. He released her, taking a step back so their bodies were no longer touching.

A warm evening breeze moved within the space that was created.

"I'm sorry. I must be overtired—"

Brenda smiled and shook her head. There was no need for him to apologize. She'd needed that. Needed to feel, for one precious moment that she was attractive to another human being.

She knew this wasn't going anywhere. It couldn't for so many reasons. "You don't kiss like someone who's overtired."

She didn't look angry. Hell, she didn't even look surprised. Had she sensed it was coming? With effort, he pulled his thoughts together. Since she wasn't offended, it was best to hurry away from the incident as quickly as possible.

Dax nodded toward her car. "You'll be all right getting home?"

He was retreating, she thought. She supposed that was a good thing, but there was a small part of her that had wanted the kiss to go on. To strip her of every thought until all that was left was a raw need to find fulfillment in lovemaking.

God, but she was tired. Brenda tried not to laugh at herself.

"You dazed me, Detective Cavanaugh, but you didn't daze me that much." She flashed a smile at him. "I'll be fine," she assured him.

As she began to drive away, her eyes on her rearview mirror and the man who watched her retreat into the night, she wasn't one hundred percent sure of herself. She felt shaky inside, as if every single one of her molecules had been taken apart and then put back together again. Quickly and maybe not so precisely.

Brenda took a deep breath. Maybe it was her current emotional state that was doing this to her. The emotional state that felt in complete upheaval not just because of the kidnapping, but because she was pregnant and her hormones were just now beginning to stop playing ping-pong all over her psyche.

Hands tightly gripping the wheel, she stared straight ahead. She made every single light and found herself pulling up into her allotted parking space less than twenty minutes later, her head crowded with thoughts, with memories.

She remembered the morning she'd finally given in and marched herself down to her gynecologist where she'd heard what she already, in her heart, knew to be true. She was having a hard enough time dealing with the thought of what being pregnant represented. She'd always loved children, there was no doubt about that. But the children she interacted with all went to their homes at the end of the day. They only required so much from her emotionally. Being a mother, moreover bearing Wade's child, that was something else again.

The tiny being growing inside of her didn't change anything, really. She still wasn't in love with Wade, never had been, she thought, letting herself into the darkened apartment. But now there was more to think of than just herself, or even Wade. There was a child being brought into the world through no fault of its own. It deserved the best advantages. That meant a real home. Not the kind she'd had, with only one grudging parent in attendance, if he could be called that.

She remembered the gnawing feeling at the pit of her stomach when she'd come to her conclusion. Knowing that she had to really make a go of her marriage. For everyone's sake. Wade still wanted her. He'd made that clear throughout the long weekend they'd spent together. And every child wanted to have a "normal" family: a mother and father within sight of one another.

She paused before the refrigerator, taking out the container of milk. Reaching overhead, she took out a glass from the cabinet, narrowly avoiding hitting the container of prenatal vitamins. She kept them where she could see them, so she couldn't forget to take them every morning. These days it felt as if her mind was scattered in a hundred places.

Just like it had felt as she began to place her call to the base that afternoon to tell Wade that he was going to be a father. But before she had finished hitting the numbers on the keypad, there was a knock on her door. Two solemn-faced marines stood on her doorstep, telling her that they were very sorry to have to inform her that her husband had been killed in a freak accident during regular maneuvers.

The news had left her feeling completely hollow. She felt caught in a tailspin. After thanking them for coming in person, she'd shut the door on them and their offers of help and retreated to her bed, where she'd stayed for two days, wishing the world would swallow her up.

But it hadn't.

At the beginning of the third day, she'd crawled out of her bed, out of her shell, and got back to the business of living again. She tried to find the bright side the way she always did. She told herself that at least now she wouldn't have to be caught up in an emotion-sapping marriage, didn't have to pretend to be happy when she wasn't.

But oh, the thought of facing motherhood completely on her own scared her beyond words.

For the time being, she'd kept the news to herself, not letting any of the teachers at the academy or even Harwood himself know about her condition. She couldn't find the words to tell them. Not until she had some kind of firm plan.

In the meantime, she'd lost herself in the task of teaching the children in her first-grade class, being all she could for them. That meant opening up new worlds for them and in some cases, as with Annie, it meant opening up feelings.

But now the tables were turned and the teacher found herself being the pupil, she thought, rinsing out her glass and putting it on the rack to drain. This tall, dark detective with the dimples had opened up an entire new box of feelings for her. Reminding her what it felt like to feel.

No, there'd been more than that, Brenda thought as she made her way to the bedroom, kicking off her shoes as she went. This was more like what she'd once thought a kiss would be like. Something to erase the nail polish right off her toes.

The first time Wade had kissed her, she'd waited for the lightning, waited for that wild, heady feeling she just knew had to be part of the process. But it had never come. And eventually, she'd told herself that she'd expected too much. Reactions like that only happened in the movies, not in real life.

Except that now it had.

No, she told herself firmly, it hadn't. She slipped out of her clothes and into the worn running shorts and T-shirt she slept in. What had happened had been more than liberally helped along by her heightened emotional turmoil. It wasn't real. It couldn't be. Because if it was, someone would have kidnapped Detective Dax Cavanaugh and run off with him a long time ago, tucking him into a private cave where only they could have access to him.

She threw her clothes onto the back of a chair. Tomorrow she'd have enough energy to put them in the hamper, but not tonight.

A sensation shimmied over her. Brenda closed her eyes and relived the moment his lips had touched hers. The man's mouth should be registered with the local authorities as a lethal weapon.

Her eyes opened again and she shook her head. She was tired, stressed out, she silently insisted as she lowered herself into bed. It had been one hell of a day. By morning, things would feel as if they were almost back to normal.

It took a long time for her body to stop humming.

Morning didn't feel normal.

She'd spent a restless night, tossing and turning. Sleep, when it finally came, had been inky and dreamless. And far from refreshing.

When she woke up, the first thing that popped into her brain—exploded would have been a more apt description—was that Annie Tyler was missing.

The thought throbbed in her head as she hurried through her shower and then into her clothes. A sense of urgency pervaded every fiber of her being even though she wasn't sure just where it was she was hurrying to. She knew that Simon Tyler—Annie's father's jet had to have touched down by now—probably wouldn't welcome the sight of her any more than her mother did. But the kidnapper had said he was going to call there today and she needed to be there. For herself and more importantly, for Annie. If only just in a silent capacity, standing on the sidelines. She seriously considered taking a leave of absence to focus full time on finding Annie.

She looked at the boxes of flyers she'd brought into the house last night. Dax had said something about her using them as an excuse to gain entrance to the mansion.

Why not? It was as good a reason for her to come by as any. They couldn't refuse the flyers. Chances were, they hadn't had a chance to think about that yet. Shock had a way of blanking out your mind, she remembered.

Forcing down a piece of toast and a cup of coffee that would have been more useful for patching gaping holes in the driveway—decaffeinated in deference to the baby—Brenda picked up the boxes and headed toward the door.

She was almost out of the apartment before she remembered her prenatal vitamins. With a sigh, she doubled back. She'd never been much for taking vitamins herself, but this wasn't for herself, this was for the baby. She wanted to make sure she did everything right while she was carrying around this tiny passenger inside her body.

She used milk to wash down the vitamins, making a face as she did so. She'd never liked milk, not even as a child. "I hope you appreciate all this," she murmured to her stomach just before she picked up the boxes again.

She was on the road within a blink of an eye.

There were police cars parked up and down the winding driveway in front of the mansion. If they were meant to hold the media at bay, they weren't entirely successful. Vans representing all the major local stations were camped before the mansion as well, waiting for a glimmer of one of the main players in this real-life drama.

Frustration ate away at Brenda. From the looks of it, several vans had been there through the night, hungry for a new tidbit to throw to the detail-hungry audiences. This was a circus, she thought.

Snaking her way through the various vehicles, she looked around for someplace to park. She recognized Dax's unmarked sedan almost instantly.

He was already here, she thought.

All the way over, she'd tried not to think of him. Which caused all her thoughts to center on the man. Over and over again she kept telling herself that last night had been the result of a combination of stress and vulnerability. And besides, men just didn't fall all over themselves to be with a woman who was pregnant with another man's child. Granted, she wasn't showing yet, but she would be. By and by she would be.

Her waist had already thickened by half an inch, despite her bouts of morning sickness. Now that they appeared to be a thing of the past, she knew her body was going to begin to assume a ripening shape. How attractive was that to the average man?

Oh, but Dax Cavanaugh was anything but average.

She upbraided herself for letting her thoughts get tangled again. Okay, so he'd shaken up her world, but, like life in the aftermath of an earthquake, it had to go on.

"Sorry, you'll have to turn around, ma'am. This area's restricted."

Blinking, she realized that she'd stopped moving as she looked for an available space, and a policeman had ducked his head into her car on the passenger side. He looked as if he was running very short on patience. The officer probably thought she was part of the media, Brenda realized.

She said the first thing that came into her head. "I spoke to the kidnapper yesterday." Belatedly, she realized that had a rather crackpot sound to it. "I'm Annie Tyler's teacher." The policeman continued to look dubious. Brenda looked toward Dax's car again. "Ask Detective Cavanaugh. He'll vouch for me."

For a second, she thought the policeman was going to refuse and demand she leave. But then, with a sigh he pressed down on the button on his walkie-talkie, backing away from her car as he did so.

"Wait here," he ordered sternly.

Because he was standing directly in front of her car now, there was nothing else she could do. "I'm not going anywhere," she promised.

He lowered his voice, murmuring something into the mouthpiece. Within two minutes, she saw the front door to the mansion opening. All around her, she both saw and felt a heightened anticipation as the members of the fourth estate moved forward as one.

Instead of one of the Tylers, considered far and wide to be one of Hollywood's golden couples, or their lawyer, it was Dax who emerged from the sprawling building. Looking neither left nor right, he ignored the media and walked directly toward the policeman. And her.

Obviously the officer had given him coordinates ahead of time, she thought. Either that, or the man had an uncanny homing device to go along with his uncanny lips.

Get a grip, she warned herself.

"It's all right, Hadley," Dax told the policeman as soon as he was within hearing range.

Then he stopped and looked into the car. A din of noise accompanied him and she realized that there were reporters hurling questions at him while scores of cameras rolled in hope of securing something new, something exciting.

Dax grinned at her, causing her pulse to skip a beat or two before suddenly launching into four-four time. "I was beginning to think you'd changed your mind." He pointed to a place on the far left, close to the building. "Park over there."

Nodding, she did as he told her.

All last night, after she'd driven away, he'd tried not to give Brenda too much thought, concentrating instead on the case and what they had so far. But the sensation he'd experienced kissing her, no matter what kind of a spin he kept trying to put on it, insisted on popping up again and again, taking his system hostage each time. Vividly replaying itself all through his body.

Whatever the reason, there was no denying the fact that the lady had shaken him up. He knew he wanted a second go-around, if only to see if what he'd experienced the first time was just a figment of his overstressed imagination, or if he'd actually felt what he'd felt.

But right now, there was something more pressing

to take his attention. He walked up to her vehicle just as she got out. He noticed that she'd brought the flyers with her.

"Get any rest?" he asked as he took the boxes from her hands.

"Not much," she admitted, keeping her voice low. Wanting to keep her response away from the prying ears of the media.

How did people in the public eye stand it, she wondered. How had Annie stood it, the few times she'd been allowed out with her parents? She was such a shy little girl, she must have been terrified to have these one-eyed beings invade her world.

He used his body to shield her from the cameras trained in their direction. "Me, neither."

Brenda paused to look at him. It wasn't clear to her whether he was telling her that the case, or what had transpired between them, was the reason for his flirtation with insomnia.

But there was no way she was about to ask, if for no other reason than it seemed disrespectful to Annie and what she was going through. So she decided just to assume he was talking about the case.

"No new clues came in?"

He indicated that she should walk in front of him to the house. She realized that he was shielding her and flashed a grateful smile at him.

"A few hundred loonies have already called in," he told her. It hadn't taken long for the deluge to begin. "Every case that gets on the news attracts them."

She tried to decipher his meaning. "But you have to go through each one, just in case there's a germ of truth to it, right?"

He nodded grimly. "Right."

Luckily, he hadn't been one of the people manning the phones. Since he was the primary on the case, he could allocate that job to others. He'd put in his time on other cases and had quickly come to the conclusion that he hated being behind a desk, hated having to deal with what he felt were the sidelines. He liked being out in the field, sifting through the evidence or potential evidence firsthand. Being on top of things. There was nothing like it. He'd never been one to take life in small doses. And standing on the sidelines was enough to drive him crazy.

Which was why he empathized with Brenda York. He could see the frustration in her eyes when she thought about being kept from the front lines. For now, since she was helpful, since she might prove to be further useful, he saw no reason not to keep her in the loop.

Opening the door for her, he ushered her inside the mansion and past a distraught looking Martha Danridge, who in Brenda's estimation looked even paler than she had yesterday.

Even before they took one step toward the living room, Brenda could hear the sound of raised voices. Or rather, one raised voice. Simon Tyler was making his grave displeasure known to anyone within earshot. If the look on Martha's face was any indication, the very sound threatened to bring down the mansion's walls.

"Just what the hell are you people doing to find her?" Simon Tyler was demanding of Nathan when they entered the room.

Dax's partner looked amazingly unruffled and calm in the face of the storm he was weathering. "Mr. Tyler, we already explained that we have—"

"I don't want words, I want action," Simon bellowed. "I want Annie found. I want every inch of this city covered until you find my daughter, do I make myself clear?"

For Brenda, the show of parental concern was a matter of too little too late. Why didn't you show her you cared this much when she was here?

The words burned on her tongue. Brenda bit them back, knowing she couldn't say anything. Knowing that this wasn't the time, but still thinking that it would have done Annie a world of good to feel, just once, that her father actually cared about what happened to her. It might not have changed a single thing that was happening now, but it would have been good for the little girl to know nonetheless.

She couldn't help wondering how much was really concern for Annie and how much was anger because something of Simon Tyler's had been taken.

"We're already doing that, Mr. Tyler," Dax told the man as he entered the room.

Simon swung around to face Dax and Brenda. His

eyes narrowed, as if he was trying to deduce her identity as he looked at her.

"Who the hell are you?" he demanded.

Rebecca turned her head from the cushion. She'd been lying on the sofa the entire time. Her eyes were bloodshot, as if she had spent the night crying. Brenda felt guilty over the condemning thoughts she'd had about the woman. Maybe, beneath all her carelessness, Rebecca Allen-Tyler actually cared about her daughter.

Sitting up from her reclining position, she swung her legs down to the floor, her hands gripping either side of the sofa. Her eyes were accusing as she looked at the person her husband was addressing.

Rebecca's attractive face tightened into a scowl. "That's Brianne something-or-other. The woman who lost Annie."

Chapter 7

"Brenda York," Brenda corrected the woman without missing a beat. Despite her efforts to the contrary, she'd never met Annie's father before. "My name is Brenda York, not Brianne and I'm your daughter's teacher, Mr. Tyler."

Simon glared at her before turning to Dax. "What is she doing in my house?" he demanded.

"She ran off flyers to help find your daughter." Dax set the boxes down on the coffee table, then took off the lid from the one on the top.

Simon barely glanced at the exposed flyers. "I can have someone at my studio run off ten thousand of those," he snapped dismissively.

It was evident that Simon Tyler was accustomed to instilling fear into those around them. Equally evident was that Dax was far from intimidated, or impressed. If anything, he was struggling to hold his annoyance in check.

"The point is, Mr. Tyler, it's already done." Brenda had the distinct impression that Dax was being protective of her. It left her a little in awe as well as striking a receptive chord within her. She couldn't recall the last time someone had been protective of her. "She's also the one who spoke to the kidnapper yesterday when they called."

Simon turned toward his wife. It was well known that he didn't like being caught unprepared and this piece of news had done just that. "I thought you said that Martha spoke to them."

Rebecca looked bewildered as she shook her head. "I told her to."

Dax cut in before they could get sidetracked. "Your housekeeper was afraid she'd say something wrong." He nodded toward Brenda. "Mrs. York stepped in and pretended to be her. It's because of her quick thinking that we got the kidnapper to agree to give us proof of life."

"Proof of life?" Rebecca repeated numbly, her eyes widening with barely controlled fear.

"It means they have to give us proof that your daughter is still alive," Nathan explained. "Like a photograph with her holding up a current newspaper with the date exposed."

"You mean you think she might be—" Unable to finish, Rebecca covered her mouth with her trembling hands and began to sob. "Oh God, Simon, what if she's—she's—" The sobs grew louder.

After a beat, her husband went to her, putting his arm around her shoulders. They looked like any two parents, caught in the vice of a terrible tragedy, not the golden couple envied by so many.

Brenda looked at Dax. The photograph had been his idea, not hers. Why was he telling them that she was the one who'd thought of it? Was he trying to make them bury their initial animosity against her? Strictly speaking, she knew that the kidnapping wasn't her fault, but the Tylers certainly thought so.

The detective was going above and beyond the call of duty, she thought. Her eyes conveyed as much to him. As they met his, Dax merely lifted one shoulder in a slight, dismissive gesture.

Commiserating with the woman's anguish, Brenda was quick to tell her, "He's calling today with details where we can find the photograph. That means Annie's still alive."

Still sitting beside his wife, Simon looked up sharply at Brenda. "He?" he echoed. "Then the kidnapper is a man?"

Dax took over. "We're not sure. The voice was filtered through a synthesizer."

Impatience stamped Simon's handsome features. His scowl deepened. "Do you have any leads at all?"

"We're pretty sure it's a couple who came to your daughter's school yesterday morning," Dax told them. "Asking for a tour of the place."

"'Pretty sure.'" Simon spat out the words mockingly. "But you don't know."

Dax struggled to hold on to his temper. It wasn't the first time angry victims jumped all over him. But it did make his job harder. "The address the couple gave the headmaster turned out to belong to a recycling plant, so I'd say right now they're our best bet."

The director looked unimpressed and frustrated. "And just where is this 'best bet' right now?"

Dax measured out each word, knowing ahead of time how it would be received. "We don't know."

Simon got into his face. "Well, damn it, find them! Find them before—"

The ringing telephone made the rest of his tirade disappear.

Everyone froze, all staring at the telephone.

Simon moved to pick up the receiver, but Dax caught his wrist before he could lift it from the cradle.

"What the—"

Dax waved his hand at him, looking toward the technician closest to him. The latter was set up next to the phone with a portable telephone that had been brought in and hooked up. The man nodded and Dax released Simon's hand.

The instant he did, Simon yanked the receiver up, pressing it to his ear. The technician had shadowed his every move. The machine was recording. Calibrating.

Dax indicated that Simon tilt the receiver so he could hear the conversation firsthand. Simon glared, but complied. He held the mouthpiece firmly with both hands.

"Hello?"

"Quite a lot of excitement you have going on there, Simon. I can see it all right here on my TV. You're the breaking story on all the channels." The disembodied voice on the other end chuckled. Broadcast, the tinny sound rattled in the room. "A regular media circus. But then, you Hollywood types welcome that kind of thing, don't you? The press, the attention, it's what you live for."

"Where's my daughter, you worthless lowlife?" Simon demanded.

"All in good time, Simon, all in good time. I must say, I liked your housekeeper better. She kept her temper." There was a significant pause, as if the person on the other end was debating continuing with the conversation. "Is she around?"

Simon drew himself up to his full six foot stature. He gave the impression of being taller because he was so thin. "You'll talk to me."

"No," the voice contradicted, "I'll talk to her. Or I won't talk at all. Learn to bend, Simon, learn to bend." The pseudo-friendly tone faded. "Now do I talk to her, or not?"

Dax waved Brenda over, indicating to Simon that he should give her the receiver. Brenda caught herself thinking that if anyone's look could turn a person to stone, Simon's glare would have been the one. Finally, he shoved the receiver into her hands.

She was quick to make her presence known. "Hello?"

There was an audible sigh on the end. "Better, much better. I don't like anger," the kidnapper informed her. "It makes me dig in my heels. And that won't be good for anyone, would it?"

"No." Out of the corner of her eye, she saw the tech nician by the table indicating that she should stretch the conversation out and keep the kidnapper on the line for as long as possible.

As if in tune to what was going on, the kidnapper picked that moment to say to her, "Oh, and tell them not to waste their time trying to trace this. They're not dealing with a novice. The signal's all over the map and besides, this is a public phone. Even if they did have the mental capability of finding their faces while staring into the mirror, by the time they locate this, I'll be far away from here."

"I'll tell them." Looking toward the technician, she shook her head. The man continued trying to pinpoint the trace. "Where's the photograph?"

"Direct. I like that in a woman." The metallic chuckle scraped against her soul. It took effort not to shiver. "You'll find the photograph in the ladies' room of Hamburger Heaven. It's taped to the inside of the lid of the tank."

It was one of the most popular fast food chains around. She knew of at least half a dozen in the city and knew there had to be more. "Wait a minute, which Hamburger Heaven?"

"Mayflower and Azusa. I'll be in touch." The line went dead.

She surrendered the receiver to Dax. The latter looked at the technician. "Anything?"

The man took off his headphones and tossed them on the table. "He bounced the signal all over the country. We were closing in, but—" He shook his head.

"He's shaking his head. What does that mean?" Simon wanted to know. "What's next?"

The technician popped the audio tape out of the machine and handed it to Dax, who turned around and gave it to Nathan. "Detective Brown takes the tape into the lab for analysis and I go to retrieve the photograph." He was already crossing to the room's threshold.

Brenda stepped in front of him. "Let me come with you." Before he could refuse, she said quickly, "If the kidnapper's watching the restaurant, he might expect the housekeeper to be the one to come for the photograph. She and I resemble each other a little." It was a long shot and she knew it, but there was this overwhelming need inside her to make herself useful.

Dax hesitated. He could always use a policewoman, but that would require having the woman get a change of clothes and time was at a premium. The faster they moved, the more likely they were to recover the little girl alive. Of late, they'd been lucky with their recovery record when it came to kidnapped children and he wanted to keep it that way. He could almost feel the seconds ticking away.

"All right," he agreed. From across the room, he could see the quizzical look Nathan was giving him. "She has a point."

Nathan spread his hands, as if he wasn't about to say anything to contradict him.

Leaving his wife's side, Simon was on his heels. "What am I supposed to do?"

Dax turned at the front door. "Sit tight and wait for the call. He might decide to call while we're out getting the photograph. I think this guy enjoys pulling strings and watching people jump." It seemed as apt a description of the function of a director as any. A thought occurred to him. "He seemed especially pleased at turning the screws to you. Anyone in particular have it in for you?"

Behind them, in the living room, Rebecca rose from the sofa. Taking a step toward them, she dried her eyes. "How much time do you have?"

He hated making promises he couldn't keep, but he knew that parents of kidnapped children needed something to hold on to. "Successful recoveries varying—"

Rebecca shook her head, her auburn hair shifting from side to side like a luxurious shawl. "No, I meant for Simon to give you a list of people who have it in for him. My husband's very powerful in this town, that means he has a lot of enemies."

Terrific, Dax thought. Nonetheless, he made a mental note to show the director the sketches Brenda had made of the two people. Maybe they'd get lucky and the man'd recognize one of them.

* * *

"He'd have less enemies if he wasn't such a jerk," Dax said to Brenda several minutes later as they left in his car. Nathan was already on his way back to the precinct with the audio tape. With a great deal of luck, the lab could clean it up sufficiently to yield some kind of background noise that they could use to pinpoint the kidnapper's location.

Excitement was vying with her baby for space in her stomach. God, she hoped she wouldn't get sick. "Less what?"

Dax rolled the windows up to cut down on the noise in the form of questions being hurled at them as they drove by the reporters and their camera crews. "Enemies."

"I think a man like that counts the number of enemies he has as a testimonial to his power. The more he has, the bigger he is." She shook her head as they cleared the estate. "I never understood that kind of thing, being proud of who hated your guts."

Dax laughed. "Some people thrive on that. Me, I'm with you."

I'm with you. She knew it was silly, but she liked the sound of that, even though in reality, it meant nothing. He wasn't "with" her in any true sense of the word; it was just a figure of speech. But for a fleeting moment, she pretended that they were a unit. And she supposed in a way, for the duration of this case, they were. For as long as he allowed it.

"I think the kidnapper I talked to was definitely a man," she confirmed.

He turned toward her as they came to a red light. "What makes you so sure?"

"He said something about liking direct women. It's the kind of flippant line a guy might say."

The light turned green. Dax shifted his foot back onto the gas. "Is that the kind of line guys gave you?"

"Guys didn't give me lines." She saw him raise a quizzical eyebrow. "I never really hit the dating circuit." Her father had kept a tight rein on her all through school, demanding she be there to make his meals and take care of the house. "I was married at a young age. Right out of high school."

That would have made her, what? Eighteen? Much too young in his opinion. She'd hardly been more than a baby. "You must have really been in love to get married that young."

It would have been easier to say yes and leave it at that, but she hated lies, even little white ones. They'd been the kind she'd lived with for most of her marriage. Pretending to be in love when she wasn't. There was a huge difference between loving and being in love.

"No," she corrected, "What I really wanted was to leave home." And Wade had been her ticket. "Wade was a marine, that meant travel. Or so I thought." Things never quite turned out the way they were planned. "As it was, I never left the state. But Wade did. He was sent overseas on four tours of duty, always to places where bringing a wife along wasn't feasible."

That was why there were times when she'd hardly felt as if she really was married. She did a lot of growing up in those seven years.

Squeaking through a yellow light, he glanced at her. "So what did you do while your husband was over there?"

"Went to school, broadened my mind." Her mouth curved. "Played house." That's what it felt like because there was hardly ever a husband to sit opposite her at the table. "Got used to living on my own for the most part." She looked at his profile. It seemed so chiseled, so forceful. In a way, he looked like more of a marine than Wade had. "Found out to my surprise that I could."

"I think you could probably do anything you set your mind to."

A compliment. Lord, when had she last heard one? Wade wasn't given to wasting words and before that, there'd been no one to say anything kind to her at all. "I could have used you years ago, when I didn't believe that."

He picked up on what wasn't being said. "But now you do?"

"For the most part." Except in those wee hours of the night or morning, when everything was covered in darkness and it seeped into her soul, making her doubt herself. Making her afraid.

Turning into a strip mall, he brought the car to a stop in the small lot that looked out on three fast-food restaurants. Hamburger Heaven shared a sidewalk with Chinese-Food-To-Go and Hot Tamale. "We're here."

He held the door for her as she walked into Hamburger Heaven. The fast-food restaurant was thinly populated this time of the morning. The quick breakfast crowd was all but gone and it would be several hours before the early lunch crowd arrived.

There was only one person behind the counter. She looked from Brenda to Dax, an eager smile on her young, unlined face. Her fingers hovered over the digital register. "How can I help you?"

"Where's your ladies' room?" Dax asked.

Leaning over the register, the young girl pointed to the far side of the counter on her left. "Just follow that to the end. Rest rooms are right there," she informed them brightly.

Brenda was already hurrying down the narrow hall, leaving Dax in her wake.

"Damn it, wait up, Brenda! I'm the cop here, not you."

She pretended not to hear him. Her heart was racing. Dax was half a step behind by the time she reached the ladies' room.

"Police," he called out in case there was someone using the facilities. But there was no response. No one was inside.

He took the lead. The moment they walked inside, the smell of liberally applied disinfectant assaulted his nose. The cleaning woman had obviously just been here.

Three stalls lined the back wall. The center one

had an Out Of Order sign on it. When he pressed his palm against the door, it wouldn't give. It had been locked from the inside. Playing the odds, he went to the first stall. The door swung open and he lost no time in picking up the lid. Nothing. Brenda crowded in behind him. He heard her sigh of disappointment.

The third stall yielded the same results. Either the kidnapper was playing them, or the photograph was in the middle stall.

Dax tried the door again. It didn't budge.

"I can crawl under it," Brenda volunteered.

But he waved her behind him. "Stay back." Bracing himself, he lunged at the door, applying his shoulder to it. The door flew open as pain shot through his body. He paid no attention to it.

Brenda pushed passed him. Holding her breath, she gingerly lifted the lid from the tank and turned it over. She wasn't sure what she was going to do if there was nothing there.

But there was.

"Oh, thank God."

There was an instant photograph of Annie taped to the underside of the lid. It was wrapped in a plastic bag. Dax lost no time in removing it.

Standing on her toes, Brenda looked around Dax's shoulder at the photograph. Annie was sitting on a bed in a bedroom that looked like a thousand other bedrooms. Brenda could feel her heart tightening in her chest. Poor baby. "She looks scared."

He thought of the photographs Brenda had shown

him of the girl in her album. "But none the worse for her ordeal." The little girl was holding up this morning's newspaper. That meant that as of this morning, she was still alive. Something caught his eye. He looked closer. "I didn't realize she wore glasses."

"She just recently got them," Brenda told him. She remembered how insecure Annie had been, afraid that the other children would call her cruel names. Brenda had sat with her, mentioning other people who wore glasses as children, people who had gone on to make an impression in history. "She's nearsighted." Her eyes narrowed. "Wait, isn't that something reflected in her glasses?

It was what had caught his attention. "Looks like it, but it's hardly more than a speck."

Excitement began to build inside of her again. They had something, she could work with. "You'd be surprised at what you can see in a speck."

He made his own deductions from the tone of her voice. "Can you make this any clearer?"

"Odds are pretty good." But everything she needed was back at the academy. "I'm going to need to cross the yellow tape again. The school's got all the state of the art software," she reminded him.

That had been her excuse for crossing the restricted lines yesterday. He was far from computer savvy and had no idea what they had at the precinct. He knew one thing, though. The techs wouldn't let him hover and look over their shoulders. Brenda would. She had no choice. "C'mon, let's go."

Walking out into the dining area, Dax stopped to glance at the menu. The same girl was behind the counter, still looking eager to serve them.

He turned to Brenda. "Have you had breakfast yet?"

"Burnt toast."

He thought of the huge breakfasts his Uncle Andrew liked to prepare. On any given day, there was anywhere from five to twenty people sharing the meal with him. He'd purchased a specially made table just to accommodate everyone. The funny thing was, like the Greek fable, Uncle Andrew never seemed to run out of food. There was always more.

He knew his uncle would have been horrified at what he was about to do. "Let me get something to go for us, it looks like it might be a long morning."

Her stomach rumbled in response. "Fries, see if they have fries ready yet."

He looked at her dubiously. "For breakfast?"

She had a craving, but she didn't want to call it that. It was far too much of a giveaway. "I've always liked fries."

Actually, so had he. Dax grinned and nodded. "Okay, fries it is."

He turned toward the girl behind the counter and placed their order.

Chapter 8

Dax flipped his cell phone closed, ending the call he'd placed to Nathan. The lab was still attempting to clean up the audio tape. Stripping away the layers of synthesized interference took time. So far, nothing useful had surfaced, but Nathan promised to be in touch once it did. In the task force area, his partner informed him, the volume of calls coming in had increased. Leads were being followed, no matter how slim or far-fetched.

Before checking with Nathan, he'd called the Tylers, letting them know that Brenda and he had gotten the photograph of their daughter and that the little girl was still alive and apparently well.

Tyler had told him they planned to go on the air this afternoon to plead with the kidnapper. Dax had a feeling that it wouldn't do any good, but he kept his opinion to himself.

Behind him, Dax could hear the rhythmic tapping of keys. Brenda had taken a seat at the most sophisticated-looking computer the second they'd entered the academy's state of the art computer lab. The keys hadn't stopped clicking since she'd sat down.

He crossed to her. She hardly seemed aware that there was anyone else in the room, her attention was so rabidly focused on the monitor. She'd scanned in the picture they'd retrieved from the bathroom at the fast-food restaurant and she was in the process of magnifying and cleaning up the tiny speck reflected on Annie's glasses.

He thought of his own approach at the keyboard. Three fingers, a maximum of errors. For him, the computer had been no improvement over the ancient electric typewriters that had graced the precinct when he'd first joined the force.

In contrast, Brenda's fingers flew over the keyboard. "You really know your way around all this stuff, don't you?"

"Hmm?" Lost in thought, it took a second for her to hear his words. "Oh, yeah, I do."

The speck had begun to take on a shape, but her head was starting to ache from staring at it so much. Brenda paused to massage her temples.

"I fell in love with the first computer I ever saw. We didn't have one when I was growing up. My father didn't see the point of it since it couldn't cook or clean.

And computers didn't interest my husband, but the second I got into a classroom, I knew I had to have one." She smiled, remembering. It had been like opening up a whole new world to her. "I've tried to stay on top of things as far as progress in the computer industry goes." Glancing toward him she grinned. "It's both my hobby and my passion, I guess. I like the challenge."

Turning back to the computer, she straightened. Her back systematically cracked in three places, one after the other. She could feel her headache spreading down her spine.

Dax saw her rotate her shoulders. The movement reminded him of a sleek jungle cat stealthily making its way through the brush. She did it again. Because he had nothing else to do, he came up behind her and began to knead her shoulders. He felt her instantly tense under his hands. Gently but firmly, he held her in place when she tried to get up.

"Just trying to help you work the knots out of your shoulders." He laughed shortly as he continued kneading. "I've felt more relaxed rocks than you."

"Work many knots out of rocks do you?" It was hard not to groan the words out. He was hurting her, but at the same time, she could feel some sort of release. The tension wasn't exactly flowing out of her, but what he was doing was definitely helping ease it. "Is this what they mean by exquisite pain?"

The only context he was familiar with when it came to "exquisite pain" was lovemaking. His mouth curved.

"I don't think they were talking about shoulder massages at the time."

Since Brenda seemed to be able to take it, he slowly increased the pressure he was applying. She winced once, but she didn't complain. She had grit, he'd give her that. The lady was a lot tougher than she looked. Probably carried all her tension around in her shoulders as well as on them.

"I'm surprised you haven't broken into a hundred little pieces by now."

Considering what she'd been through in her life, so was she. But she kept that to herself. There was no reason to share it with a stranger, no matter how magical his hands might be.

Brenda shrugged. "I guess I'm a type A personality."

She didn't have to tell him that, he'd already surmised as much. "You should think about being an A-minus once in a while." The stiffness wasn't abating, even a little. "Damn, I've worked on some hard knots before, but I think you take the prize."

For her part, she struggled not to let her eyes slip shut. This really did feel good. "You moonlight as a masseur?"

"No moonlighting, but my cousins and brothers hit me up every so often for a good massage." Janelle referred to him as "iron hand" and refused to let him come anywhere close to her, but Troy and Jared swore by him. "Stress of the job," he explained.

She would imagine that being a policeman had to

be very stressful in a city like Aurora. They had their share of crime. "So who does you?" The question came out before she could think to stop it. She bit her lower lip. He probably thought she was trying to pry into his personal life.

"I don't get tense." That wasn't strictly true and he amended his statement. "At least, not to where it makes me walk around like a wooden soldier."

She took no offense. After all, if nothing else, wooden soldiers had great posture, right? But she was curious about something.

"You don't get stressed?"

"Sure." Taking a smaller amount of muscle between his thumb and forefinger on either side of her neck, he squeezed, then began to massage again. Finally, the knots grew smaller. "You can't work this job and not get stressed."

"Well, then?"

Moving in a downward pattern, he pressed his palm against her back. Brenda tried not to sigh. "I find other ways to release the tension."

"Oh." An image of Dax, his limbs tangled with those of some nubile, raven-haired woman, suddenly flashed through her brain. "Sorry," she murmured, shifting uncomfortably. "Didn't mean to pry."

Realizing what she had to be thinking, Dax laughed. Yes, he did alleviate some of the tension he felt by temporarily losing himself in fast, nonbinding relationships that lasted slightly longer than a dandelion in bloom. But that wasn't something a man mentioned around a woman, at least not unless he was setting ground rules. He wasn't sure if he wanted to set any rules here, or even if they were necessary. This was a whole new place he found himself entering.

Besides, it wasn't what he meant. "I swim and I work out regularly."

She had no idea why that made her happy. Or why it ushered in a feeling of relief. She only knew she could feel her mouth curving. "That would explain the upper body strength."

"Come again?"

To explain, she reached over her shoulder and placed one of her hands over his. "It feels as if you actually could pulverize those rocks you mentioned."

"Oh." He stopped massaging her shoulders and took a step back. "Sorry. If it was too hard, why didn't you say something?"

She didn't want to tell him his hands on her felt like heaven. So she gave him what had become her standard excuse. "Because my father taught me not to complain."

Because if she had, he'd only hit her harder. So she'd learned to bite her lip and take it, mentally taking herself off somewhere else and vowing to leave the first real opportunity she found.

And Wade had been it.

"Was your father a military man, too?" Dax asked. Her husband had been a soldier. Maybe she was drawn to a man in a uniform because she wanted to please her father.

"No, just a frustrated bully who didn't like to hear crying."

Pausing, he turned her chair around to look at her, making the natural deduction. "You cried?"

She didn't like being put under a microscope and examined. But she couldn't find the words to tell him to back off. Maybe in part because she didn't entirely want him to. "I learned not to."

"Or else?"

"Or else," she echoed. Those were her father's words. *Or else I'll whip the flesh right off you.* It wasn't something she cared to go into. What happened to her within those four walls where she'd grown up was something she never talked about. In the beginning, she'd wanted, at least just once to unburden herself. But Wade hadn't wanted to listen, saying the past was best left behind her and that there was nothing to be gained by bringing it up and reliving it. So she'd let it die.

Except that it wouldn't.

It came back to her in dreams sometimes. She'd see her father looming over her, a belt in his hand, yelling at her to be quiet even as he whipped her over something she'd done, or had forgotten to do.

Or for something that someone had done to him.

She learned quickly enough to make herself scarce after serving her father supper.

Brenda pressed her lips together. "Let's just leave it at that."

He looked at her for a long moment. This conversation was getting way too serious. That was usually his signal to back away. The less he really knew about a woman, the less likely he was to get tangled up with her. But there was something in Brenda's eyes that kept him from his usual dance. "You know, I'm a pretty good listener."

Any minute now, she was going to say things she was going to regret, open doors she wanted to keep closed. She needed to distract herself. So Brenda turned her chair around, back to the desk, and started working on the image on the screen. She tried to sound amused, detached. "Are you, now?"

He placed his hand on her chair. "Yes, I am."

She was aware that his fingertips were just a hair's breadth away from the side of her neck. The sensitive side. She strove to keep things light. "And just what is it you listen to?"

"Anything you might want to tell me." That wasn't enough and he knew it. She seemed adept at finding loopholes. "Anything you might need to tell me," he amended.

Turning her head, she looked over her shoulder, expecting to see a flirtatious grin on his lips. Instead of a grin, she saw a smile. An encouraging smile. As if he meant what he said and he wanted her to take him up on his offer.

But the words were so deep down inside of her now, she didn't know if she could drag them up.

"Nice to know," she murmured. "Thanks for the

massage." She moved her neck from side to side. "It feels much better."

He'd only scratched the surface. "Good."

An image of giving her a full body massage materialized in his mind. He banked it down. Something was humming between them, he realized. Something he couldn't put a name to or identify. Something he wasn't even sure he liked, but it made him curious and he'd never been able to back away from a puzzle. It was what made him good at his job. But once the puzzle was solved, he moved on. That's what made him lousy at relationships.

Brenda hit a few more keys, striving to clean up the image she'd enlarged. It was still fuzzy, but she'd finally brought it to a level where the speck now had a form.

And it was a female form.

She tried one more time, enlarging it further. Everything lost its perspective. Brenda hit another series of keys, reforming lines and parameters. She stared at the face that had emerged on the surface of Annie's glasses. "It's her."

Dax leaned over her shoulder, his hand braced on the back of her chair as he stared at the less than pristine image. "Her?"

Her heart hammered harder. Whether it was because she felt they were getting nearer to finding Annie, or because he was standing so close, she didn't know. "The woman who was at the school."

He turned her chair around so that he could look at her. "Are you sure?"

Brenda blew out a breath, trying to be as truthful as possible. "Could I differentiate between her and her twin sister, or a lookalike cousin? No. But barring that I would say that the woman there," she moved her chair back around so that she faced the screen again, "definitely bears a striking resemblance to Mrs. Kingsley, the woman I was giving the tour to when the fire broke out. And Annie disappeared."

That was good enough for him. "Can you remember if she was with you at all times?"

She shook her head. "All I remember was focusing on getting the children out," she said honestly. "I really don't remember where she or her husband were during all this, but I'm fairly certain that they were—" Her eyes widened as a thought materialized. "Wait a second, the girls' bathroom."

Was she talking about the bathroom at the fast-food restaurant? Had she seen something there that he'd missed? "What about it?"

But she was talking about the bathroom at the school. "The woman asked to use it just after we started the tour. It was right after we came out of the music room. She wasn't gone long." Certainly not long enough to arouse any suspicion. "But she joined us in the art room and I didn't think anything of it. We were on our way to the library when the alarm went off."

It was falling into place now. "That was probably

when she started the fire," he told her. "When she supposedly went to the bathroom."

She frowned. "In all the excitement, I forgot about that." Brenda was annoyed with herself. He'd asked her questions, why had that faded to the recesses of her mind until just now? "Damn it, I should have remembered that."

So far, she'd been nothing but a huge asset. She was being much too hard on herself. "Don't beat yourself up about it, you remember it now."

Brenda blew out a breath. "Right, for all the good it does."

"It establishes a time line," he pointed out. Dax knew how frustrating it had to seem to her, but this was the way things worked in the real world, things didn't come together in a rush. It was usually one piece at a time. "Every clue, however small, helps to give us a whole."

"You do fortune cookies, too?" The second the words were out, she regretted them. "Sorry, that sounded kind of snippy, didn't it?"

"Not when it's followed by an apology. You've been through a lot."

Emotionally, she'd been through the wringer. And her attraction to Dax, not to mention being pregnant didn't exactly help things along. "Not as much as Annie has."

There was no arguing that, but getting mired in thoughts of what might be happening to the little girl, even as they stood here talking, wouldn't help free her.

They had to keep their efforts focused on the goal. He nodded toward the enlargement on the screen. "Can you print that up?"

"No sooner asked than done." Brenda hit Ctrl P and the printer spit out an exact copy of what she had on the monitor.

Taking it out of the tray, Dax studied it. It was still somewhat fuzzy. He raised his eyes to hers. "Can you clean this up any more?"

Brenda shook her head. "Not without being creative and enhancing it. This is still the image. Anything I come up with beyond that could be subjected to interpretation."

"Good enough. This just confirms our theory that the couple kidnapped Annie." There was no doubt in his mind that if the woman was standing there watching, the man had to be one taking the picture.

Dax saw the doubt on Brenda's face. "What?"

Funny how things began to come together. First the memory of the woman stepping out for a moment, now this. "I saw both of them once we were outside the building. They came and told me that these were less than ideal conditions for them in which to view the school. They said that they'd be back when things settled down."

He followed her line of thinking. "So what you're saying is how could she have taken Annie and still be there to talk to you?"

Brenda nodded. "Can't be in two places at the same time." She chewed on her lip, thinking out loud.

"Maybe in all the chaos that followed the alarm going off and the fire engines arriving, one of them managed to get Annie to go with them and stashed her."

"And what, came back later to get her?" That didn't seem very feasible to him. "You said you combed the school."

Against the orders of the firemen, she'd run into the building, screaming Annie's name. She ran through the entire first floor, but Annie hadn't been there. While she'd been doing that, Annie could have been taken somewhere else.

"Maybe not thoroughly enough."

He had another idea. "And maybe there's someone else involved."

Brenda rose from her chair. "You mean one of the teachers?"

His eyes were on hers. "Do you have any better ideas?"

It seemed like the logical way to go, but he and his partner had ruled the teachers out. "But you already questioned them."

"So we'll question them again." It wouldn't be the first time a felon managed to slip by without detection. "More closely this time."

The school was supposed to open again tomorrow. It was going to be difficult enough to go about business as usual without having the police there again to requestion everyone and remind them of Annie's kidnapping. "They'll think you suspect them."

"Then they'd be right," he told her simply. He saw

the surprise on her face at his bluntness. "I suspect everyone until proven otherwise."

She pressed her lips together, then asked, because she had to know, "Even me?"

The smile took over his lips very slowly. "No, not you."

She believed him. But again, she had to know. "Why not?"

This time, the smile gave way to a grin. "Call it a gut feeling."

She'd heard that cops often relied on their gut instincts, but had thought that was just another myth. "And what kind of an average does your gut have?"

He had this sudden urge to kiss her. Definitely bad timing. But because he thought it was best to play it safe right now, he shoved his hands deep into his pockets. "Oh, about ninety-seven percent of the time."

"Ninety-seven percent wrong or ninety-seven percent right?"

He laughed. "Ninety-seven percent right." He grew serious. "Do you want me to suspect you?"

"No, of course not." She was relieved that he still didn't, even though he was retracing his steps deductively. But that didn't change the way she felt deep down. "It's just that I feel so responsible for this."

Dax put his hands on her shoulders, anchoring her in place so that she couldn't try to escape his words. "Listen to me. You didn't do anything wrong. You had, how many kids to take care of?"

"Twenty."

"Twenty." He nodded. He would have been undone by more than two. "Twenty kids you had to get out of the building—"

And she'd failed. "I only got out nineteen," she reminded him.

His eyes searched her face. "You always this determined to take the blame?"

Brenda shrugged off his hands and turned away from him. She crossed to the window and looked out. The computer room faced the front of the building. Where they had all gathered to get away from the fire that had been little more than a hoax. The front lawn looked so empty, so desolate to her now.

"Habit," she murmured.

He's struck a nerve, Dax thought. But he couldn't get himself to back away. "Husband?"

Brenda wrapped her arms around herself. She felt suddenly cold. "What? No, Wade never blamed me. He was a good man."

So she kept saying. Was it to convince him, or herself, he wondered. "Then who?" Dax pressed, coming up behind her. "Your father?"

Her eyes met his in the reflection. She forced a smile to her lips, reminding herself that the way to face the ordeal of Annie's kidnapping was to be upbeat. She had to believe they would find the little girl. Otherwise, she was never going to get through it. "Let's see, masseur, philosopher, shrink—" She turned around to face him again. "Anything else?"

"Police detective," he said. "Don't forget police detective."

And that, he thought, was his cue. Whatever feelings this woman aroused in him, they were going to have to take a back seat to what was important right now. Finding Annie Tyler.

He picked up the image Brenda had printed up. "Let's get this to where it'll do the most good."

"Sounds like a plan." Brenda paused only long enough to remove the photograph from the scanner and shut down the computer.

They hurried out of the building, unaware that someone was standing at a window on the third floor, nervously watching them leave.

Chapter 9

"Please bring my baby back. Please call and tell us what you want and where you want us to leave it so that we can get Annie back."

Rebecca Allen-Tyler was doing what she did best. Playing to the cameras. Evoking emotion from her audience.

Brenda stepped back as she looked at the scores of representatives of the news media, who were all crowded around in front of the table where Simon and Rebecca were set up. The long table was littered with microphones, their metallic heads turned upward so not to lose a single syllable. The impromptu press conference had been called less than three hours ago and the citizens of the fourth estate had been summoned to the Tyler mansion to carry the broadcast.

Brenda scanned the area around the couple. There wasn't a non-empathetic face in the crowd. But the woman wasn't really playing to the media. She and her husband were playing to an audience of two who were watching somewhere. Watching and gaining a great deal of satisfaction? She couldn't help wondering if Rebecca and Simon were doing exactly what the kidnappers wanted them to do. Begging.

Still, in Rebecca's position, she would have probably done the same thing. Who knew, maybe the kidnapper did have a heart somewhere in storage and this would bring it out. She glanced at Dax at her elbow. "Think this'll do any good?"

He'd been against this, but it wasn't exactly his call. Besides, the ball had already been rolling by the time he arrived at the mansion.

Standing off to the side, he could only preside over the proceedings. "You mean appealing to the kidnappers' sense of decency? No. But this is probably giving them exactly what they wanted. A sense of power. Of control." He frowned, lowering his head to reach her ear so that his voice wouldn't carry and interrupt the broadcast. "Rebecca Allen-Tyler is literally begging to get her daughter back. She's letting the kidnappers know that she'll pay any price. If one or both of them are after control or revenge, it's got to be a good feeling for them."

"What if it's Simon they want it from?" Annie's father sat solemn-eyed beside his wife. His lean face looked haggard. He had said very little, for once leaving the words up to his wife.

Dax saw him the way he imagined the kidnappers would see the man. "He looks pretty beaten up. I'd say that probably feeds their ego, too."

A commotion at the table drew both their attentions back to the man they were discussing. Simon had pulled one of the microphones even closer and was talking into it, interrupting his wife. His anger was almost a tangible thing.

"Call, damn you. Stop playing games with us, with our daughter and call. Tell us how much you want and where you want us to bring the damn money." His impatience and frustration was clearly registered there for anyone to see. Flashes went off and cameras whirled, recording the moment, the passion.

The overwhelming signs of barely suppressed panic.

Dax shook his head. "He just handed everything they wanted to them."

Brenda didn't want to think that way. "But if the kidnappers want the money—"

"Oh, I don't doubt they want the money," he assured her. "But they want the drama, too." As Simon exploded for the camera, Dax drew her back even further from the eye of the storm. "Don't forget, this is California. Where every second person either has a screenplay they've written or a pile of eight by ten glossies sitting in the top drawer of their desk."

"I don't," Brenda quipped.

He only smiled at what he found to be her innocence. For such an independent woman, she did have a naive side. The woman continued to surprise him. "I said every second person."

She pretended to count, silently pointing a finger first at herself, then at him. "That would be you." When he made no hurried denial, she realized he was speaking from experience. Brenda tilted her head, studying him. "Let me guess. Screenplay?"

"Notes for one," he corrected. His grin was quick and easy, and gone within less than a minute. "But that's not for public knowledge."

He hadn't really told anyone else about it, not even his cousin Shaw who was, all things considered, his best friend. But there seemed to be no harm in letting the information slip out. Brenda wasn't really part of his world, at least not a permanent part who could use this information against him and tease him at will, the way his cousins or siblings could.

Or Nathan for that matter, he thought. His mouth curved again. Nathan's idea of writing was signing his weekly paycheck.

Wow, you just never knew about a guy, did you? Detective Dax Cavanaugh would have been the last person she would have thought capable of having the patience to sit down and hammer out a screenplay.

"My lips are sealed," she promised.

His eyes were drawn to her mouth as if to verify her statement. He thought of last night and felt a quickening in his body that was completely out of place in the given situation. Out of place or not, he found himself wanting to kiss her again.

"Keep them that way," he instructed in hushed tones.

Before them, the media surged forward. The excitement of the moment, along with its charged, heightened emotion was quickly making the situation dangerous and possibly volatile. It was time to cut the press conference short.

Dax stepped forward, becoming official again. He waved the reporters back. "Okay, everybody, you've got your story and your sound bite. Now everyone please clear out so we can go about our work."

As one, the reporters refocused their attention and turned toward him. Questions were fired at him from all directions. "Detective, have you made any progress?"

He refused to answer that, knowing that anything he said would be diluted and distorted.

"Any truth to the report that Annie was spotted in Taos, New Mexico?"

"We're checking it out," he responded to the disembodied question while motioning to the patrolmen at the back of the room to usher the media out the front door.

"Is it true you suspect one of the teachers?" someone else shouted. Variations of the question echoed throughout the crowd.

"We're still in the process of ruling out suspects," Dax responded.

"How about her teacher, has her teacher been ruled out?" someone else asked.

Though she was behind him at the moment, he could feel Brenda watching him. "Yes, Mrs. York has been ruled out."

"How about the headmaster?"

"We'll let you know as soon as we have anything," Dax promised. The combined effort of the three policeman had the crowd finally crossing the threshold and on the other side of the front door. Dax closed it with feeling. "When hell freezes over," he added under his breath as he turned from the door.

Simon and Rebecca were still standing in the living room, both shaken, both holding one another for mutual support. Dax looked at Simon. "You shouldn't have done that."

Instantly, Simon took umbrage. His pale complexion darkened. "I can't just sit here."

Didn't the man get it? According to Nathan, the director was sharp. Supposedly he'd graduated near the top of his class from the University of Southern California. Why didn't book-learning translate into a drop of common sense?

"That's exactly what he wants you to do, Mr. Tyler," Dax told him, struggling with his own temper. "Sit there. He wants you to sit there and squirm while you wait for the telephone to ring."

"But why?" Rebecca asked, her voice frantic. "The sooner he calls, the sooner he can get his money."

"It's not always about the money. Even in a ransom

case," he underscored, not wanting the girl's mother to start torturing herself with other, lurid possibilities. "Sometimes the main component in all this is the power."

"Power?" Rebecca echoed blankly. She looked at her husband for an explanation.

But it was Dax who gave it. And he gave it to Simon rather than her because more and more he was beginning to believe that this had been done specifically to Simon not because he was the wealthiest parent at Harwood, but because the kidnapper wanted to extract a measure of revenge along with his money.

"Yes. You have the power of artistic life or death over the people who work on a movie with you. Maybe Annie's kidnapper wants to sample a little of the same. Maybe he's someone you slighted, possibly ruined, and he wants to get his revenge." He had picked up copies of the sketches Brenda had done on their way back to the mansion. He took them out of his pocket now and unfolded them before placing them on the table in front of Simon. "Do either of these two people look familiar to you?"

Simon glanced from one to the other, then shrugged impatiently. The next moment, disgusted, he swept the pages away with his hand. "Look, I've been in the business fifteen years. I see a lot of people. I can't be expected to remember everyone."

Dax's voice was emotionless. He could see that the man was probably a tyrant on the set, the kind more than one person probably swore to get revenge against.

"No, you can't." And maybe that was the point, however twisted it might be, Dax thought. Maybe whoever was doing this wanted Simon to remember him, remember the impact he had on his life.

Kidnapping a man's daughter left quite an impact.

Tucking the pictures back into his pocket, Dax turned away from the Tylers and began to walk out of the living room.

"Where are you going?" Simon called after him.

Dax could see how the man could easily rub legions of people the wrong way. "I've got teachers to question."

He didn't have to look to know that Brenda had fallen into step beside him. He didn't say anything to her until they were outside the building.

"Don't you have someplace to be?"

Now that he'd opened the door to allow her to be part of this investigation, however marginally, there was no way she was going to willingly be left behind. She had to at least try to accompany him.

"Not at the moment. Besides," she said, trying to bolster her argument, "you're going to need a friendly face at your side when you go at them again."

He would have described her face as something other than friendly. Enticing, beautiful were two of the words that came to mind. Dax crossed his arms before him. "You're volunteering your face?"

He was going to let her come. She relaxed slightly. "Like I said, it doesn't have any place to be at the moment."

He nodded toward his car. The media, he could see, was converging again and heading their way. "Get in then, before the sharks go at us again."

He didn't have to tell her twice.

According to the payroll statements, Harwood Academy employed seventeen teachers. Fourteen to handle their classes and three who substituted. They conducted classes that dealt either with computer science, art or music. In addition, there was one librarian, a woman who had been with the academy ever since the first headmaster had opened the school's doors some fifty-one years ago.

"Came to work at Harwood fresh out of college," Amanda Brooks told them proudly, walking back into her tiny, knickknack-crowded living room.

She set down the tray she'd brought in from the kitchen and presented a tall glass of lemonade to each of them before taking one herself. With a contented sigh, she sat down on a comfortable, slightly shapeless chair and faced them across a scarred coffee table. One of her three dogs came to place its head on her feet.

"I don't get much company," she confided, looking down at her dog. "They tend to be kind of shy around people. Butterscotch and Taffy are hiding in the bedroom, but Caramel tends to be the curious one."

She paused to scratch the dog's head, then raised her eyes to her guests. "Nothing like this has ever happened at the academy before." She leaned forward, her body language announcing that she had a secret to share. "One of the teachers had to leave in the early sixties because she got in the family way. She was a single lady, you understand." Amanda shook her blond-tinted hair in mute disapproval. Whether over the teacher or her subsequent censure was unclear. "But other than that, there hasn't been a hint of a scandal. Until now." She sighed over the rim of the glass before taking another long sip. "I don't know what this is going to do to enrollment."

"And you saw nothing out of the ordinary yesterday?" Dax pressed.

Amanda drew herself up and sat ramrod straight. Brilliant blue eyes stared at him accusingly from behind rimless glasses. "A fire is out of the ordinary, Detective."

"But there really wasn't any," he reminded her gently. "Just someone setting Mrs. York's wastepaper basket on fire."

"A fire's a fire, big or small." Primly she nursed her lemonade before speaking again. "As to anything else out of the ordinary, I wouldn't know about that. I was too busy making sure that the youngsters in the library all got out all right. That, and saving Edna."

"Edna?" He hadn't heard the name mentioned before. Was it a student of some special significance? He looked from the librarian to Brenda for an explanation.

Because Amanda appeared to be preparing for an unabridged version, Brenda quickly explained, "That's what Amanda calls the first edition book we have. It's a volume of poems—"

"By Edna St. Vincent Millet. My gift to the school after I was here for twenty-five years," the older woman told him with no small amount of pride. "I found it in a small secondhand bookstore in London. My husband took me there for our second honeymoon. He died two years ago last spring. Butterscotch and Taffy wouldn't come out from under the bed for days. I don't know what I would have done if it hadn't been for Caramel…"

They weren't going to get anywhere here, Dax thought. He realized the woman needed to talk, but he didn't have time to listen. He set his glass down on the coaster Amanda had placed before him.

Amanda ceased her narrative. "Are you leaving so soon?" Disappointment dripped from her words, and she rose to her feet along with them. Roused, Caramel yapped her displeasure and then retreated to her resting place.

Dax looked as apologetic as he could. "I'm afraid we have a lot of other people to talk to."

"I understand perfectly. Never do anything by half measures, that's always been my motto." She accompanied them to the front door, opening it for them. "Will the school be open tomorrow?" Amanda's bright blue eyes watched him hopefully.

Forensics was finished processing the area. The yellow tape across the front entrance was coming down later this evening. "Yes."

Amanda nodded her approval. "Good, I don't like having too much time on my hands. Makes me lazy."

She caught Brenda's arm just before the latter crossed her threshold. Brenda looked at her quizzically. "He's a nice young man," Amanda whispered. And then she winked and closed the door.

Dax looked behind him as Brenda hurried to catch up. "What was that all about?"

Brenda grinned. There were times when the librarian didn't appear to be playing with a full deck, but she suspected that the woman was just amusing herself. She seemed as sharp as any of the younger teachers. "She thinks you're a, quote, 'nice young man,' unquote."

Dax laughed as he opened the driver's side door. "I am." And then he looked at Brenda over the vehicle's roof. "For the most part."

A slight shiver shimmied up and down her spine. She looked at him in wonder—and amusement. "Detective Cavanaugh, are you flirting with me?"

He pretended to consider her question. "I don't know. Maybe." He got into the car. "I'll get back to you on that."

Brenda followed suit, shutting her door. She had to press her lips together to keep the grin from taking over her entire face.

They saw ten more teachers that day, but it quickly became evident to Dax that there was no new information, no forgotten scrap of a clue to offer. And, more importantly, no feeling in his gut that he had stumbled on to something.

The teachers, all women, struck him as dedicated and eager to do whatever they could to help with the investigation. But no one had seen anything in the least helpful to that investigation. And no one could be sure just where the couple that Brenda had been showing around was at any given time once the fire alarm had gone off.

Ordinarily, he would feel that time was growing short. Which meant that it was running out for both the investigation and for the kidnap victim. But, if his theory was correct, then there was the kidnapper's ego to factor in and that might be enough to buy them a little more time.

He glanced at his watch as they left the last teacher of the day. It was getting late.

"Wait a minute," he told Brenda as she began climbing back into the car.

She paused, waiting for an explanation. Instead of giving her one, he punched in several numbers on his keypad. Brenda listened in silence as Dax checked in with the patrolman he'd left in charge at the Tylers' mansion. She watched his face in the light from the street lamp and drew her own conclusions.

"Nothing?" she asked the moment he flipped his phone closed.

He shook his head. "Nothing. There's been no contact made." Annoyed, frustrated, Dax tucked away his phone. "It's as if the kidnapper is trying to see how far he can stretch Tyler's nerves before they snap." He got into the car and snapped in his seat belt. "Either that, or he's changed his mind about the money."

She quickly got in on her side, shutting the door a little too firmly. "But they're worth billions. If you had a chance at that, would you walk away?" He raised his eyes to hers sharply. She hurried to clear the air. "I meant, if you were the kidnapper?"

It hadn't been that long ago that his cousin Patrick had been under investigation by Internal Affairs. It had been guilt by association but there was no telling where it would have led if the woman carrying out the covert investigation hadn't quickly become convinced of Patrick's innocence. Suspicions were a sore spot they were all forced to live with.

"No," he replied firmly. "But I'd have to be getting nervous about getting away with it. There are going to be a lot of eyes focused on that bag of money when it finally gets left for pick up," he pointed out.

"Maybe the guy thinks he's more clever than the police. You know, maybe he fancies himself some kind of criminal mastermind. Pride Goeth Before a Fall, and all that sort of thing."

She had a point. More than one criminal sitting in a state prison had been instrumental in tripping himself up because he underestimated the police and overestimated his own resourcefulness.

"Maybe," he agreed.

Angling his watch, he tried to make out the face. It was almost nine o'clock. There was no point in going back to the Tylers' tonight. The atmosphere there had to be nothing short of incredibly tense.

"You hungry?"

Other than the fries he'd grabbed at Hamburger Heaven this morning for breakfast, they'd stopped at a drive-through for sandwiches around noon. But right now, that felt like a hundred years ago.

As if in response to his words, she thought she heard her stomach rumble. Brenda pressed her palm against the area. Now that she no longer began each day with a ten-minute purging session on her knees in the bathroom, she had rediscovered her appetite, which had always been a healthy one. Prior to her unexpected pregnancy, she'd always been blessed with a metabolism that emulsified food almost before it hit her stomach. She wondered if being pregnant was going to change that.

"I could eat," she allowed.

A horse, if that rumbling of her stomach was any indication, he thought with a grin. "So could I. How about a place where we don't have to lean over a metal counter to place our order?"

"You mean a real restaurant?" She grinned when he nodded. "Sounds good to me."

It did to him, too, Dax thought as he started up the engine in his car.

Chapter 10

"So, tell me about this screenplay you're writing," Brenda said in between bites of a chicken quesadilla that was so good, it was carrying on an open flirtation with her taste buds.

Dax couldn't help thinking his uncle Andrew would really like this woman. She did enjoy her food. "I told you, I'm not writing it, I'm just putting notes together, that's all."

She raised her eyes to his. He was being deliberately evasive. Had she found a weak spot? He seemed so confident otherwise. "But notes mean that you intend to write it."

"Someday," he qualified, "when I'm old and gray and I'm on the sidelines because they won't let me play anymore."

Brenda paused to take a sip of soda before asking, "Is that how you see it? Playing?"

He was quick to correct the frivolous impression she'd obviously gotten of his approach to crime. "Being a player rather than someone on the outside. The game of life can be very serious."

Her eyes narrowed as she absorbed his words. "So life is a game?"

He shrugged. Things were serious, but you couldn't take them too seriously or they would paralyze you if something really went wrong. "It depends on how you look at things. In a way, everything's a game. There are always winners and losers."

"How about just content people?"

"Those are the winners."

"I see." Brenda rolled his words over in her head as she savored her meal. And then she smiled. "You are a philosopher."

He shook his head. Philosophers were people who went around and around about things, ending up nowhere. He was just telling her what worked for him. "Just somebody with a healthy attitude, that's all."

She laughed. He was deeper than he looked. "I'd like to see those notes of yours someday."

Dax took her at her word. He paused to think it over, then shrugged carelessly as he went on eating. "Sure, why not? After this is over."

After this is over.

Did that mean he wanted to see her once he had put this case behind him and there was no need for them to interact? Or was he just making polite conversation, giving her a throwaway line the way people did when they didn't know what to say?

Looking at him, she couldn't tell. She felt too drained to try to come to some kind of reasonable conclusion tonight. But it did have a nice sound to it.

She changed the topic, returning to what was on both their minds. "You know, this is pretty nerve-racking, not having him call after we got the picture." She ran her teeth along her lower lip, working at her words, her concern. "Do you think something happened?"

Dax broke off another piece of bread and ate it without butter. "I'd be lying if I didn't say that was a possibility."

Trying to gauge his tone got her nowhere. "But you don't think so?"

"What I think is that the kidnapper is enjoying torturing Tyler."

It was far the lesser of the two evils. But she needed reasons, something she could believe in beyond her own prayers. "What makes you so sure?"

"Because otherwise, he would have already named the drop-off point." He noticed she'd finished her soft drink. Raising a hand, he signaled to the waitress, then pointed at Brenda's glass. The woman nodded and hurried away. "Most kidnappers—if they're not snatching a kid for perverse reasons or because they want a kid of their own and don't have one for one reason or another—want the whole thing to be over as soon as possible. They want to get their hands on the money."

The waitress returned with a fresh glass, exchanging it for the almost empty one in front of Brenda then retreated. Brenda waited until she was gone before continuing.

"Since you think he wants to hurt Simon, do you think…" The words refused to come in an orderly fashion, jumbling on her tongue. She tried again. "Do you think that he'll return Annie to her family?"

He heard the emotion in her voice, saw the tears suddenly shining in her eyes. His gut told him that the answer to her question was no and that she knew it as well as he did. The ultimate revenge on Tyler would be to make him twist in the wind, then collect his money and still do away with the little girl.

But Brenda wasn't asking for him to confirm her fears. She was silently asking him for something to cling to.

"Most people don't want to kill," he told her, leaving the borders deliberately vague. "Especially not a defenseless little girl."

Brenda stared at her glass, watching the drops of moisture chase one another down the side, forming small rivulets.

Most people.

He'd gone from the specific to the general. She knew it was the best she could hope for. That, and maybe a miracle. She nodded slowly, accepting his terms. "Most people," she echoed.

As she drained her glass of soda, Dax looked at her plate. There was nothing left on it, not even the sprig of parsley. She'd certainly been hungrier than he'd thought. "Want anything else?"

She shook her head. This marked the first full meal she'd actually had since her morning sickness had stopped. It felt good to feel full without the threat of nausea taking it all away again.

But there was a tightness in her stomach that had nothing to do with morning sickness and everything to do with the situation that existed. The entire situation. Annie, the man sitting opposite her, the baby she hadn't told anyone about. Everything.

Her nerves felt as if they were on the verge of snapping apart like so many pop-beads.

She forced herself to focus only on his question. "No, this was fine. Thank you." She took a breath. She felt more stuffed than she'd thought. All too soon, she thought ruefully, she was going to look pretty stuffed as well. "I think I'd better get home."

Dax nodded. He looked around for their waitress again, holding his hand up for the check.

But when they arrived at her door, Brenda found that she didn't want to be alone. She wasn't tired anymore. The sensation of moving through molasses she'd been struggling with earlier had completely disappeared and she knew she wasn't going to be able to sleep. Most likely, she was going to spend a very restless night, thinking about Annie, about the possibilities they hadn't put into words.

Taking out her key, she looked at him. "Would you like to come in?"

There was a street lamp not fifteen feet away from her front door. The illumination pooled just before them, leaving her half in light, half in shadow. And completely enticing.

Everything within him told him that saying "yes" wasn't a good idea. That once he crossed the threshold into her ground floor apartment, he'd be crossing another threshold as well. There was no question in his mind, no doubt. It was just a given.

He could feel it in his bones, see it in her eyes.

Dax stood outside, knowing he should say something polite about the hour and about their both needing their sleep.

As if reading his mind, she said, "I don't think I can sleep."

"And you want me to bore you to death with a verbal recitation of those notes I've written for that screenplay in my distant future?" he teased.

He made her smile. More than that, for some reason she couldn't put into words, he made her feel safe. Just having him close by seemed to keep away the bad thoughts that threatened to haunt her.

"No." She looked up into his eyes. "I don't want to be alone tonight."

The honest admission undid him. Dax followed her inside.

The moment the door was closed and she turned to him, the tempo was set.

Dax framed her face with his hands and kissed her. Slowly at first, savoring the contact while still leaving her an opening. Letting her back away at the last minute if she came to her senses. Because, it was apparent to him, he wasn't going to come to his. Not with this feeling she'd generated within him. This need to have her.

But instead of resisting, instead of taking a step back, Brenda leaned into his kiss. Twining her arms around his neck, she silently surrendered herself to him.

It was all he needed.

The rest happened as if it had been orchestrated by an unseen hand that belonged to a force which was far greater than him.

The kiss deepened, taking them both somewhere outside the realm of mere human beings who sought one another for comfort within an uncomfortable world. Dax felt his body instantly ignite. He pressed her closer to him, savoring her softness, the way her body melted into his.

It was as if all this had been waiting for him, whether to tease him by saying that this was possible, or by giving him a single glimpse before irreversibly shutting the doors, he didn't know, but somewhere in his soul, ever since he'd kissed her last night, he'd known that this moment was here.

It was as close to perfect as he'd ever encountered.

His arms tightened around her as needs and urges rushed over him, demanding instant gratification. He held them off, struggling for the upper hand, struggling to go slowly because this, something whispered in his brain, this was different. This wasn't like all the other pleasurable couplings he'd enjoyed.

He couldn't explain why or how, but he just knew. This was different. And he meant to enjoy it for as long as he was allowed.

Was she crazy?

The question hammered in Brenda's head to the same beat her heart had assumed. She had no answer for that. The immediate one would have been "yes." Yes, she was crazy. Crazy for a multitude of reasons. She was pregnant, she hardly knew this man, she wasn't the type to do this kind of thing. Besides Wade, there'd never been any one else. No other lovers. It just wasn't her way.

And yet, here she was, initiating this, inviting this man into her home. Into her body. And she wasn't doing anything to stop it.

She couldn't.

She wanted this too much. Electricity hummed through her, lighting her up from the outside in. Chasing away the shadows. Filling her.

She'd felt so hollow. Long before Annie's abduction, she'd felt something was missing from her life. Perhaps had never been there in the first place. She'd hoped, prayed that being Wade's wife would fill that void. Would succeed in making her world whole.

But it hadn't. It had been a disappointment.

She was no longer physically or mentally abused,

but she was still adrift. Still alone, despite the man who slept beside her whenever duty didn't take him away.

This was different.

For the first time in her life, she felt she was with someone. She didn't feel alone. She knew it had to be her vulnerability talking, or maybe she was just out of her head. Maybe everything had conspired together to push her over the brink and she couldn't reason properly any more, but she didn't want to know the reasons, didn't want the explanations. What she wanted were the sensations that raced up and down her body, setting her on fire, making her yearn.

There was nothing and no one except this man with the magic mouth, with the enchanted hands that seemed to know just where to touch her, where to caress her. Her body hummed like an instrument long left unattended in the corner, relegated to the shadows, but was now rendering a wondrous melody.

One by one, gently and with tenderness, he'd taken her clothes from her body, in the end setting more than her flesh free. He'd somehow found the key to unlock her soul as well and for however long this lasted, she was going to glory in it.

She moaned as he pressed kiss after kiss to her face, to her throat. To the breasts that throbbed each time his lips left their mark.

Quickly, Brenda started to take off his clothes as well. In her urgency to divest him, she was aware of a button plinking down on the coffee table as it resisted her movements, falling off instead of finding its way out of the buttonhole.

"Sorry," she murmured, her mouth against his skin as she pushed the shirt off his shoulders.

Dax drew her head up, took possession of her mouth. "I have a sister who sews," he assured her, his words echoing against her mouth.

She heard the eagerness in his voice, felt the gentleness in his hands. Her body vibrated with anticipation even as her mind, what there was of it, cautioned her that there was only disappointment in the wings.

She knew that from experience, even as her body urged her on. Even as her core moistened to receive him.

Lovemaking with Wade had never been this exciting, but it had had its spark. Still, he was always finished with the journey just as she was beginning to climb up the summit. She'd never once gotten to that pinnacle she'd so often heard described.

She tried to brace herself for the letdown, even as part of her prayed that she was wrong.

They were on the floor now, where Dax had laid her down, their limbs tangled. He'd completely ignited her, his fingers deftly playing her body, finding secret places and making them his.

Her breath caught in her throat. Strumming lightly along her thighs, his lips assaulting hers, his fingers delved into the most intimate part of her. Brenda felt herself tightening like a bow. Softly, he stroked her, his movement evoking responses throughout her whole body.

She gripped his shoulders to anchor herself. And suddenly, there were stars zooming through her head, nestling in her bloodstream. Arching madly against his hand, her body taking on a mind of its own as it sought the center of the pleasure he'd created, she cried out as a climax took hold of her.

Desperately, she tried to hold onto the moment, afraid of letting it go. Afraid of never feeling its wondrous effects again.

Her eyes flew open as she felt his warm breath along her stomach. The next moment, his fingers had given way to his tongue. Indescribable sensations appeared. A cry echoed silently in her throat, trapped there.

Waiting.

And then it came, taking her prisoner, throwing her upward. Her fingers dug into his flesh until she was spent. Stunned, shaken, wrapped up in a rosy hue she'd never felt before, she tried to focus. To savor.

When she looked, he'd slid his body up over hers until his face was level with hers. There was an enigmatic smile on his lips. And a look in his eyes that she couldn't fathom either.

The next moment, he was parting her legs and driving himself into her. And then there was no more room for thoughts, no more room for anything except the delicious sensations battering her body.

She pushed her hips up, sealing herself to him, to

the tempo that he had set for them. She kept up as best she could and then she was scrambling toward something again, a sensation that beckoned to her as the urgency of his body directed her toward it.

It burst over her, cocooning her in its richness. In that moment she realized that she had finally gained the summit.

That they had reached it together.

His body lost its tension and relaxed against hers. She welcomed the weight, welcomed the feeling of being one with him in ways she couldn't begin to describe. The peace was overwhelming, in sharp contrast to her heart which she was certain was going to burst out of her chest at any moment.

And then she felt his mouth curving against her neck. He was smiling, she realized, and the sensation was wonderful.

After a beat, Dax raised his head and looked at her. He combed his fingers through her hair, moving it from her face. They were both damp with each other's perspiration. For some reason, he found that incredibly sexy.

Just as he found her.

The smile on his lips rose into his eyes. "Did I tell you I like your apartment?"

Laughter bubbled up inside of her, giddy laughter that had no rhyme or reason but felt wonderful as it filled her. "No, you didn't mention that."

The smile softened, growing into something more. "I like your apartment."

Brenda could feel herself weakening again. Wanting him again even as exhaustion threatened to claim her. "Good. Me, too."

Her lips puckered as she uttered the last word. It was too much of an invitation for him to resist. Dax brought his mouth down to hers. And felt the process beginning again.

He stayed the night.

Each time he had attempted to leave, she'd turn into him, or murmur his name, or the light scent she wore would somehow find its way into his senses, into his head and he was caught fast.

They made love twice and then he did something he'd never done before. He watched her sleep.

Something was going on and he didn't understand what or why. He didn't like going along for rides when he didn't have control of the wheel, and yet, he couldn't find it in his heart to leave. Not yet.

He was still searching for his lost resolve when he finally fell asleep.

The sound of the 1812 Overture, muted, burrowed its way into his sleep and dragged him up to the surface. Opening his eyes, it took Dax a moment to realize that he wasn't in his own bed, wasn't sitting in an awkward, cramped position at a stakeout.

He was lying beside Brenda.

The next moment, the fact penetrated that his cell phone was ringing. He turned toward the nightstand on his side, where he'd had the presence of mind to place his phone when he finally realized that he wasn't going home for the night.

The dark blue object, with both its ring and vibrate options on, inched its way to the edge of the stand. He grabbed it just in time.

"Cavanaugh."

Beside him, he could feel Brenda rousing. He glanced in her direction. Her sheet dipped on one side, exposing a breast. He felt desire taking root again, hard.

In his ear, he heard his partner's voice say, "I think you'd better get down here, Dax, and bring the teacher with you."

He sat up, combing his fingers through his hair as if that could somehow bring order to his still-sleeping brain. Morning had pushed its way into the room. His mind was a step behind.

"Come again? Why?"

"Because the kidnapper just called and he won't talk to anyone here but her. He said he'd call back and then hung up. The Tylers are about ready to leap out of their skins."

Definitely trying to get Tyler's goat, Dax thought. He scrubbed his hand over his face. "Did he say when he'd call back?"

"No, but I think you'd better get here fast. If he calls, he might not give us a third chance. No telling what this loony's going to do."

"Right."

Nathan terminated the call on the other end. Turning, Dax looked at Brenda again. His reaction was no less intense than it had been a moment ago. She looked better with sleep still in her eyes and her hair tousled about her head than most women looked in full makeup, walking out of a beauty salon.

The pull was getting stronger rather than weaker. As if he'd just whetted his appetite rather than sated it. This wasn't business as usual for him and he didn't know what to make of it, but he had no time to explore it. They had to get going.

"That was Nathan. The kidnapper called the Tylers this morning."

Her eyes were on his face, as if she was waiting for him to tell her something terrible. "So I gathered."

Sitting up, she had the sheet tucked around her breasts. He struggled with the very strong desire to tug it away.

"He won't talk to anyone but you."

Dax saw a smattering of a smile curve her lips and felt an unreasonable desire to taste it. To see if it was as sweet as it appeared. Damn it, what the hell was going on with him?

"I always did attract the wrong kind of men," she murmured, getting up, the sheet wrapped around her like a Roman toga.

As he watched her gather up her clothes and go into the bathroom, he couldn't help wondering if she included him in that group.

Chapter 11

"Tyler must be madder than hell," Brenda commented. Around them, the world was just beginning to wake up. Morning traffic on the streets was still at a minimum as they sped from her apartment to the Tyler mansion.

Dax took a sharp left, beating out the light a hairsbreadth before it turned red. "That's probably the idea, to get at him. To get under his skin."

Brenda frowned. The window on her side was down an inch and the wind was sneaking into the space, whipping her hair around. She combed it back with her fingers. "You'd think kidnapping his daughter would accomplish that."

He knew what she was saying, that the man's love for Annie should have made everything else pale in comparison. But to a man like Simon Tyler, power was everything. It was the rock that his ego, his sense of self-worth was founded on. To strip him of it was the ultimate insult. Being powerless far outweighed the taking of his money or even of his daughter.

Brenda shifted in her seat. In the ten minutes that it had taken to get from her bedroom to the car, she'd managed to put in a call to the academy and had left a message with Matthew that she wouldn't be in today. Harwood kept several substitute teachers on call. The school was scheduled to be reopened, but she doubted that all the children would be back so soon.

She looked at Dax, wondering if any headway had been made that he hadn't mentioned. "Has anything turned up on those two people who were at the school?"

He shook his head. "The names they gave Harwood were fake, so was the address and phone number where they could be reached. So far, all the tips we've had come in after those sketches of yours were shown on TV have led nowhere."

She ran her hands along her arms. The chill she felt came from within and refused to abate. "Doesn't mean we won't get a valid one."

"No, it doesn't." He spared her a glance. It was another balmy day. "You cold?"

She shook her head. It wasn't the kind of cold that an extra blanket or a sweater could combat. "Just thinking about Annie being scared, not knowing what was going to happen to her." With all her heart, she wished she could somehow hold the little girl, comfort her. "Annie's very bright for her age. She's probably thought of where this is all going."

Annie was only six. He didn't know much about kids, but that was something he would have thought more typical of an adult reaction. "That's giving her a lot of credit, isn't it? I know that people think kids have this natural intuition, but—"

He didn't understand, Brenda thought. "Annie tested near genius level when she came into the school. Her score was one point higher than mine."

She saw Dax give her a curious look.

The last part had just slipped out. She wouldn't have said anything if she hadn't been so preoccupied, hadn't felt so confused and guilty. Not just about failing Annie, but about last night as well. The lovemaking had been wonderful, beyond anything she would have imagined possible.

For the first time in her life, she'd felt that wild surge, that wondrous X-factor that had eluded her all this time. Until now. The one that was ultimately responsible for attracting a woman to a man and vice versa with an electricity that sizzled. But she was carrying another man's child and though she'd never been in love with Wade, she had loved him in her own fashion. There was no denying that she felt a degree of disloyalty to him for making love with someone else. Wade had been dead only a little more than three months.

What was worse, she knew that she shouldn't have

let things go this far without telling Dax that she was pregnant. She knew why she'd kept silent about it. Because she was afraid. Afraid that if she said anything, it would have destroyed all chances of there ever being anything between them.

Still, what made her think that there was anything between them now except that incredible interlude that they'd shared? He hadn't exactly been proclaiming his undying love to her last night. Men and women made love all the time without feeling love, she had to remember that. Just because she'd felt the earth move last night didn't mean that he had.

Last night had just been last night and today was today. She had to gain the proper perspective on that, the one she knew in her heart that Dax undoubtedly had to have had.

So, she was a brain on top of a beauty. Well, he'd already suspected as much. This was a first for him, Dax thought. The women he usually made love to usually had an IQ slightly larger than their dress size. Maybe that's what had been missing all these years. Maybe that was what pulled him back.

The road opened up and he pressed down on the gas. "You're awfully quiet all of a sudden. Is this something geniuses do?"

She flushed. It hadn't been her intention to let him know her genius level. Men were uncomfortable with women who were deemed to have an intelligence that ranked above the norm. Yet he didn't look uncomfortable, she thought, studying him. She relaxed a little.

Still, she didn't want to dwell on the slip. Instead, she told him the partial truth. "Just worried."

"Yeah, me too."

And he was. But not about what she was referring to. He was worried that the letdown he had come to expect, the one that always came soon after he had attained his goal—had slept with the woman who had caught his fancy—wasn't coming. Because if it didn't come, then he was playing a completely new ball game, on completely new ground and he hadn't a clue what was going to happen next. If he didn't know, how was he going to be prepared?

The night they had spent rode with them in the car like a huge elephant both pretended not to see.

The phone rang as they were let into the Tyler mansion. Swiftly beckoning her forward, Nathan pointed to Brenda.

She rushed into the room, but Simon snatched the receiver up before she could reach it. "Hello." The single word was a demand more than a greeting as he barked it into the phone.

"Is she there?" the tinny voice on the other end of the line asked. Despite the metallic sound, Dax could swear he could hear a gleeful note in the voice. "Your housekeeper, is she there?"

Simon's brows drew together, dark as thunder. "Yes." He jerked the receiver away from his ear and thrust it at Brenda.

Her heart took its by now familiar position in her throat. "Hello?"

"Good, he's being sensible. Rare for him."

She knew she was supposed to draw the call out, to keep the monster on the other end talking, but all she could think of was getting Annie out of wherever she was. "Where's Annie?"

"All in good time, my dear, all in good time. You know, I originally asked for two million, but that seems like such a small sum, don't you think? Especially to a man like Simon." The voice grew impersonal. "So I'm upping it to five million. Five million in unmarked, unsequential bills in two black bags that won't have powder exploding over the money the second I open them. Drop it off at Mulberry Park." He paused for a moment. "Are you familiar with the bird sanctuary in the middle of the park?"

It took her a minute to remember the park's lay-out. "Yes."

"Good. The center bench that faces the sanctuary. Leave the money under it. Bring it yourself. Two o'clock sharp."

He still hadn't said anything about the little girl. "Annie," she cried, aware that Rebecca Allen-Tyler watched her every move, her eyes haunted. Maybe she'd misjudged the woman. But how awful that her daughter had to go through something like this to make the woman realize how precious Annie was. "What about Annie?"

She heard a chuckle. Brenda's hand tightened on

the receiver, wishing it was the man's throat instead. "Don't worry, she'll be returned by and by."

Her eyes met Dax's. She knew if the bargain went this way, there was a chance they might never recover the girl. "No, she has to be returned at the same time."

"Tyler's rubbing off on you. Probably in more ways than one. Too bad. You don't make the terms. I do."

"But—"

Like a match bursting into flame, the man on the other end lost patience and viciously swore at her. "You listen to me, you do exactly as I say, or she dies. When I have my money, I'll call with the directions on where you can find her."

A dial tone hampered any protest Brenda could have made. She looked at Dax as she placed the receiver down, defeat fighting for possession of her soul. "The bastard hung up."

Dax turned to the technician positioned beside the phone. "Anything?"

The man shook his head. He looked at the path the signal had mapped out on the monitor. They were several seconds short of honing in on a location. "The guy's playing with us. He knows just how long to stay on before hanging up."

Dax nodded, expecting nothing less. "His game, his rules." He looked at Simon. "Can you raise five million dollars before two o'clock?"

Money was never the problem. Simon impotently shoved his hands into the pockets of his designer slacks. "My bank's been alerted and is on standby."

Blowing out an angry breath, he turned on his heel, heading for the study. "I'll let them know what I need."

The man was talking about it as if it were mere pocket change, Dax thought. He could see why the kidnapper was attempting to humiliate him. If his goal was meant to incorporate personal humiliation, then treating Simon as if he were a useless underling was the only way. The key to getting to Tyler was certainly not his money.

Dax nodded at the information. "Have them get the money here as fast as possible." He turned to look at Nathan. The latter knew what they needed to do. This wasn't their first ransom drop off. "We can have one of the policewomen do the drop off—"

Brenda pushed herself into his line of vision. "He said he wanted me to drop the money off."

Dax repressed a sigh. Her feelings about the girl, or his feelings about what happened between them last night couldn't enter into this or color his thinking one way or another. And there was something more at play here than her just being a civilian amateur in this.

"He doesn't know what you look like," he pointed out. "He does, however, know what Mrs. York of the Harwood Academy looks like. If he sees you there, he might bolt." His voice softened. "No slipups, Brenda. We can't afford it and it's not something you want to live with."

"I need to be there, Dax."

He was already taking out his cell phone, calling for backup. There was surveillance to set up, police personnel to get into undercover disguises. Mulberry Park was the main park in the city. It was where everyone who wanted to commune with nature went. That meant there was a cross section of the city's population in the area. It gave them options.

He couldn't find it in his heart to tell her to stay here. But she had to be clear about this. "You can come in the car with me," he told her.

Across the room, he saw that Simon was in the study, on his phone. Calling the bank to have them prepare the money. The kidnappers had to be pretty happy with themselves, Dax thought. They had everyone, including Simon, jumping through hoops.

The question was, would that be enough? And would they ultimately let the little girl go?

He couldn't let himself think about that. He stuck to getting the pieces into place.

"How many of these people are with the police department?" Brenda murmured to Dax through barely moving lips.

At five minutes to two, they were sitting on a park bench, close enough to the drop-off point to be able to quickly sprint in if and when the need arose. Dressed in casual clothing, they were playing the part of a young couple with eyes only for one another.

Under any other circumstances, Brenda thought, it wouldn't be hard to lose herself in the part. But right now, her entire body was rigid with anticipation. And fear.

The team had fallen into place quickly once word went out. If he didn't know them himself, he could have been hard-pressed to say which people were on the job and which were civilians.

Dax grinned. "Try to pick them out."

Stretching, as if she'd been sitting too long, Brenda glanced around. The scene appeared to be completely natural to her. There were two nannies, talking to each other, their charges apparently two of several who were playing in a large sandbox not too far off. A couple of tough youths, hugging skateboards and arguing over something, were to one side while a tired-looking businessman was stretched out, grabbing a little shut-eye on another bench. A couple more people stood by the sanctuary, obviously taken with the birds. One of them had an encyclopedia with them, cataloguing the various species.

She shook her head, presenting her face back to his. "I give up. How many?"

Because the part called for it, he cupped her cheek and kissed her, all the while keeping his eyes on the scene behind her head. It took a great deal of concentration not to lose himself in what he was doing. In what he was tasting.

"All of them," he finally told her.

Stunned, she glanced to her far left. There was a man in a navy-blue jumpsuit, pushing a cart before him. He paused to sweep up something. "Even the guy cleaning up?"

Dax allowed himself a grin. "Especially the guy cleaning up. That's Nathan."

She knew she couldn't stare without giving the man away. But she wanted to. "You guys are good."

"That's the goal," he murmured. About to kiss her again, Dax went on the alert.

A man on a bicycle headed their way. Wearing a helmet and a spandex uniform of black and white, the twenty-something youth looked no different than a lot of other cyclists, except that he rode straight toward the bench beneath which the bags had been stored.

Dax took a moment to smooth his collar, actually raising it to his lips. "Heads up, people, looks like this might be show time," he murmured into the tiny microphone pinned to the underside of his shirt lapel.

The cyclist barely broke rhythm as he reached under the bench, retrieved the black bags and then turned around and headed back in the direction he'd come.

No one seemed to move. At least, not after the cyclist. Hadn't they heard Dax, Brenda wondered. For that matter, Dax was still sitting there himself. Letting the cyclist get away.

She was on her feet instantly. He had to grab her arm to keep her from running after the man. "Why aren't you getting him?"

"Because we want him to lead us to the kidnapper. This guy's obviously just a flunky. Anyone who's gone to this kind of trouble has thought things out, Brenda." On his feet, Dax headed toward his car parked less than a hundred feet away. "He's on the move, people,"

he said into his lapel. All around them, the various police officers dropped their facades and began walking toward their vehicles. "Don't worry," he assured
Brenda. "We've got people on the outside of the park,
ready to follow him."

As if to confirm what he told her, his scanner
squawked to life. "Looks like he's on his way to the
bus terminal," a disembodied voice informed them.

"And so are we," Dax told Brenda as he started up
the car.

They gave the cyclist a wide berth until he'd placed
the bags into a locker located in the last row of lockers
at the far end of the bus station. He no sooner began
walking away from the locker, key in hand, when Dax
gave the word.

"Looks like this is going to take a while, guys. Grab
him."

The moment he said it, even as he and Brenda hurried over to the man, the place came alive with police.
All wore various outfits and they closed ranks around
the cyclist, pulling out their badges and letting them
hang out on plain sight as they came.

The cyclist looked completely thunderstruck. His
eyes grew as huge as two serving plates when he saw
the displayed badges and the drawn service revolvers
that went along with them. Despite the disbelief on his
face, his hands went straight up in the air in surrender.

"Hey, what is this?" he cried. "Some kind of
prank?" Hands still raised above his head, he looked

from side to side as if he was expecting one or more of his friends to pop out of the wings, laughing with triumph as they pointed at him.

"If it is," Dax promised, "you just might wind up wishing you were never born." Gun still trained on the cyclist, Dax nodded toward two of his men. "You and you, stay here, keep an eye on the locker. The rest of you, come with me." He made eye contact with Brenda and nodded in response to the silent question in her eyes. She could come with them to the police precinct.

"But I didn't do anything wrong," the cyclist cried, tugging against the cuffs that had been slapped on him. "This is all a mistake."

"We'll see," Dax promised grimly, leading the way out of the terminal.

The cyclist, looking as if he were on the verge of a nervous breakdown, clung to the story he'd given them the instant they were in the interrogation room. He looked at Dax, repeating the words not like a man who'd memorized his alibi, but a man who was terrified of being convicted of something he hadn't done.

"A guy in a bar told me I could make an easy two-hundred dollars if I picked up a couple of bags for him and delivered them to the locker at the bus depot. I'm out of a job, so I said okay." He took a breath. "No," he repeated before the detectives in the room could ask him again, "I don't know who he is. I never saw him before. He gave me the money and then left."

Dax looked at him skeptically. "And he trusted you."

The cyclist, booked as John Michael Powell with no priors, shrugged his shoulders. "I guess I've got an honest face."

Dax leaned into him, his face inches away from Powell's. "And a non-functioning brain. How did you know that what you were transferring weren't illegal drugs?"

The cyclist stared straight ahead. "I didn't." And then he twisted around to look at the other two men in the room. "Look, if I'm guilty of anything, it's being stupid. I don't know what this is all about."

Exasperated, Dax slid the sketch Brenda had made in front of the man. "Did the guy in the bar look anything like this?"

Relieved to finally be believed, Powell stared at the sketch for a long time. When he raised his eyes, he looked hesitant. "Maybe. But he had a mustache and he talked kind of funny. Like he had some kind of an accent. I don't know what kind. French?"

Powell looked hopefully from one detective to another, as if trying to discern if he'd said the right things, the things that would set him free.

Actors had access to makeup, Dax thought, looking down at the sketch again. The kidnapper could have made himself up to look like anyone he wanted. And that also meant he could have been somewhere at the bus depot when they were there, watching them without their spotting him. Dax had a sinking feeling in the pit of his stomach.

"Can I go now?" Powell pleaded. "I told you all I know."

"We'd like you to be our guest a little while longer," Dax said. He took his jacket from the back of the chair. "I'm going back to the bus terminal," he told Nathan. The latter was still wearing the navy-blue jumpsuit issued by the city's sanitation department. He grinned at his partner as he nodded at the disguise. "By the way, good look for you."

Nathan said something unintelligible under his breath. Dax left it that way.

Brenda had witnessed the proceedings on the other side of the one-way mirrored glass. The second she saw Dax stepping out of the room, she was in the hall.

She caught up to him in two strides. "Where are we going?"

He knew better than to think he could leave her behind at this point. And if luck was with them and they captured the kidnapper—since the two men he'd left at the terminal hadn't called to say anyone had come to take out the contents of the locker—he wanted her along to help calm the little girl. Provided the stars were all aligned correctly and things went their way for a change.

He kept trying to focus on the positive and ignore the gnawing feeling at the bottom of his gut.

"Back to the bus terminal," he told her. "I've got a hunch."

Brenda found that she had to lengthen her stride to keep up. The man's legs were longer than they looked. "About?"

The thought of keeping her in the dark crossed his mind fleetingly, but she was so in tune to all this, he let the notion drop. "I hope I'm wrong, but I've got a feeling that our kidnapper might have been there all along, watching us watching his messenger."

"And?"

"And," he said, pressing the button for the elevator, "there was a hell of a lot of confusion when we came down on the guy he sent."

She tried to cling to the positive. "But you left two policemen back there. They were supposed to watch the locker."

That didn't change what he felt. "Yeah, but there was a small window of time opened when nobody was watching anything but all of us were converging on Powell. If the kidnapper is as good as I think he is, that was all the time he needed."

She stepped into the elevator and took a deep breath. "I hope that for once, your hunch is wrong."

"So do I," he told her grimly as the doors closed. "So do I."

Chapter 12

Brenda looked around Dax's arm into the metallic space that had just been exposed. The space was as large as the hole in the pit of her stomach.

The din around them in the bus terminal had faded to a dull background noise. "I guess this doesn't mess up your average."

Dax had gotten the bus terminal's general manager to open the locker in question. The man stood to one side now as they looked in to find that the black bags Powell had deposited were gone. Just as Dax's gut had told him, the kidnapper had used the momentary confusion with the cyclist to make off with the money.

The two plainclothesmen he'd left watching the locker both shrugged helplessly as they looked on.

"Nobody came near it, Detective, I swear," the younger of the two told him.

The officer beside him nodded in confirmation. "We watched it the entire time. Nothing. People came and went, but nobody stopped."

"Well, they didn't just disappear by themselves," Dax barked, frustrated. He looked at the manager, a short, bald man with a wisp of a mustache under a large nose. "You have surveillance cameras here?"

"Just a couple." He pointed first in one direction, then another. "One by the ticket counter, one by the lockers."

There was no point in bothering with the camera located over the ticket counter. "I want to see the tape from the one by the locker."

"This way."

The manager brought them to a small room off to the side which could barely accommodate Dax, the two officers and Brenda, much less the small man sitting at the two monitors.

Dax glanced toward Brenda, but her expression told him she was staying where she was. He let her remain and turned toward the manager. "Wind it back to two o'clock and go from there."

It wasn't long into the tape that Dax had his answer. Watching, one of the officers beside him swore under his breath. While the police surrounded Powell, an average-sized man wearing a San Francisco Giants jacket and a Giants baseball cap pulled over his eyes opened the locker in question, took out the bags with the money and then closed the door again, locking it.

He quickly disappeared out of camera range.

Brenda looked at the clock in the lower right-hand corner of the tape. "Gone in under sixty seconds." She turned her eyes toward Dax. "Now what?"

He blew out a breath. Damn, but he'd wanted to be proven wrong. Just once, it would have been nice if something went off according to plan. "Now we go back to the Tylers and tell them that we lost the guy who kidnapped their daughter."

She felt for him. Felt for all of them. It was easy to see from their expressions that everyone associated with the case was personally involved. It was hard not to be. "Isn't there anything else?"

Dax felt like he was staring at a blank wall. What they needed was a break, and right now, there was none in the offing.

"Follow up the leads coming in on the phone and pray for a miracle. I'd say we're overdue." He looked at the general manager. "You got a printer around here? I want a picture of that guy." He was going to have it passed around in order to see if anyone remembered seeing the man at the time in question. Maybe they could get a general description of his car.

The manager scrambled to provide a hard copy.

Once he had the print, Dax handed it to one of the two officers and gave them instructions. He wanted the general area canvassed. Maybe someone would recall seeing a man in a Giants jacket and cap, carrying two black bags, leaving the area. It was worse than a long shot but it was all he had at the moment.

Other than the grim task directly ahead of him. This wasn't as bad as telling someone a member of their family was dead, but it was a close second.

Thanking the general manager, he left his men to their work and walked out of the terminal. Outside, the air was heavy and muggy. It didn't help his mood any.

Dax paused at the car and looked at Brenda over the hood. He didn't want to drag her into this any further than she already was. "Why don't I drop you off home first?"

About to open the passenger door, Brenda stopped. "Didn't you just say that you were going back to the Tylers?"

His expression was grim as he nodded. "Yes, but you don't have to go through that with me. It's not something to do if you can avoid it."

Her eyes met his. She seemed to look right into him. "But you have to."

He shrugged carelessly, masking his dread. He'd rather chew nails than do what he had to do right now. "It's my job."

She understood that. Understood, too, that she didn't want him having to face it alone. He'd brought out something protective in her. Usually, it was a reaction she felt only for children. It almost made her smile. Wouldn't the big, strong police detective love hearing that? "You might need a buffer."

Hell, he needed more than that. Right now, he

couldn't help wanting a stiff drink and the power to will himself into soothing amnesia, at least for a few hours. But that was the coward's way out and he was a Cavanaugh. Cavanaughs weren't allowed to be cowards, or even entertain cowardly notions. It just wasn't done.

He studied her face for a moment. "I thought you didn't like the Tylers."

"I don't, but no one should have to go through this kind of thing alone."

"Can't argue with you there." Dax got into the car. He couldn't say why, but he felt oddly comforted, knowing she was going to be there with him when he delivered the news.

It was no better than he'd expected.

Simon ranted and raved about police incompetence, threatening to sue everyone, past or present, who had ever been attached to the police department. While he went on with his tirade, Annie's mother fell silent, then gave way to sobs.

She was the one Dax felt for. But his words all felt flat on his tongue as he tried to offer them to her in some measure of consolation. He wasn't good at that sort of thing, never had been.

It was Brenda who put her arms around the woman and held her as she cried. And he was grateful for her having the guts to come with him when she knew what it would be like. No doubt about it, the woman was a warrior.

"It's just a setback," she told Rebecca. "These things never go smoothly, but the recovery record has improved an incredible amount." She told her everything she could think of that might help, might give her something to cling to until this was finally over. "And Annie's very resilient. She'll keep her head about her. She's very brave and if there's a way to get away, I know Annie'll find it."

Rebecca raised her head from where she'd buried it in her shoulder. Her face was tear-stained and blotchy. For once, the woman wasn't involved with her appearance. Instead, Rebecca looked at her, her eyes searching for something. "You know her well?"

Brenda could hear the plea in the woman's voice. She wanted to be told that it was going to be all right, that Annie would come through this and that she would be home again.

Brenda nodded in response to the question. "Teachers aren't supposed to have favorites. But she's mine." As she spoke, she struggled to beat back her own fear. Giving in to it would do neither of them any good. "She's a terrific little girl who can do anything she sets her mind to."

Rebecca pressed her lips together, another sob threatening to breath through. "I hardly know her, except that she's small and mousy."

Brenda smiled with affection as she thought of the little girl. Annie was small for her age, but that had nothing to do with her inner spirit.

"Not so mousy. It's just something she does to avoid

attention. But she's been blossoming these last few months."

"And I've been too busy to see it." Rebecca grasped her arm. "I want a chance to get to know her." She sobbed the words out.

Helpless, Brenda could only hold the other woman. "And you'll get it. I promise."

"Then go do something about it," Simon snapped. Pacing, he was livid and red-faced. Gone was the un-ruffled Hollywood kingpin. In his place was a man who his legion of fans and detractors wouldn't have recognized. "Stop making empty promises." Crossing to Brenda he glared at her. "Don't think I've forgotten that this is all your fault. You should have been more careful with my daughter."

Releasing Rebecca, she stepped back from the woman, anger smoldering in her eyes as she locked eyes with Simon. It took everything she had not to tell the man exactly what she thought of him. "Maybe you should have been, too."

Simon looked as if he was going to hit her. "What the hell is that supposed to mean?"

Dax slipped in between the furious director and Brenda. "It means maybe you should calm down, Mr. Tyler." His tone was cold, warning the man to back off. "I'm having Detective Brown stay with you in case the kidnapper calls back tonight."

Deprived of his target, Simon breathed fire. "What about her?" He jerked a thumb at Brenda. "He's going to want to talk to her."

"Already taken care of," Dax assured him. He'd had the technician set up call forwarding so that any call coming in could be patched through to Brenda's cell phone if she wasn't with the Tylers at the time the kidnapper called.

In his gut, he didn't think the kidnapper was going to call, but he couldn't leave the possibility open, just in case. Taking Brenda's arm, he ushered her out of the mansion before anything else could be said.

"You okay?" he asked once they were outside and in his car again.

She fumbled with the seat belt. The metal tongue resisted fitting into the slot. She tugged on the belt again. This time, it fit. Brenda realized that her temper was dangerously short and took a second to draw in a deep breath. "Yeah, why?"

"Tyler was pretty hard on you back there."

The second he said it, she could feel herself getting a second wind.

"Oh, that." She shrugged his concern away. "I've had worse. A lot worse."

Starting the car, he backed out of the long winding driveway. "A lot of angry parents at Harwood?"

"No." She shook her head, remembering. The sadness that encroached surprised her. It had been a long time since she'd felt sad when thinking of her childhood. This thing with Annie had brought it all into vivid focus again. "Just one angry parent. Mine." She shrugged, trying to make light of it. "My father was always mad at the world and I was its representative."

His foot hovered on the brake as they took the incline down. "He beat you?"

She was about to deny it, but what was the point? It was all part of her and fortunately, in the past. "Sometimes."

Eyes on the twisted path, he spared her a quick look. "Where was children's services?"

"Servicing other children," Brenda quipped, then decided he deserved more of an answer than that. "To get into the picture, someone would had to have called them."

He didn't see why no one would have. "Nobody noticed you had bruises?"

There were no bruises visible to the world at large. "My father was very good at hitting me only where they couldn't be detected."

"How about the hospital?" It was the duty of doctors in the ER to report anything suspicious when it came to children.

He was being incredibly sweet, she thought, worrying about the girl she'd been. She found that enormously touching. Hormones again, she reasoned. But the effect was still there.

"He never broke anything so I never had to go. Besides, most of the damage he inflicted was verbal." She sighed, reliving a moment. It had been just after her mother left. He'd put the blame on her shoulders and almost succeeded in making her believe she was at fault. "He did know how to run a person down."

There was a light at the bottom of the hill. Dax

stopped there and looked at her. It was as if she was talking about someone else's past. "You don't seem any the worse for it."

One side of her mouth rose a little in a half smile. "That's because I liked myself even if he didn't. And I'd already promised myself that I wasn't going to turn into someone who was bitter, someone who could only look for answers in the bottom of a bottle."

Her father had been a drunk and both verbally and physically abusive. No wonder she'd run off with the first man who asked her. He found himself wishing that he had been the one to come to her rescue. "You're a remarkable woman, you know that?"

Her smile widened then, with both sides of her mouth fitting into it. He could feel himself becoming captivated. "Just your average, everyday survivor, that's all," she told him as he stepped on the gas again.

"Nothing average about you, Brenda York."

The sound of his voice danced along her skin, romancing her. Seducing her.

He was drawing her in. Little by little, she thought, he was drawing her in, making her believe that maybe, just maybe, things could work out between them in the long run. That he, Dax Cavanaugh, was the one she'd been looking for so long. The Prince on the White Charger was actually a cop driving a navy-blue car, but the particulars didn't matter. What mattered was that he made her feel the way she'd once believed she could feel. Wildly giddy. Empowered. Wonderful.

And how was he going to feel once he knew she

was pregnant? Assuming that he was anywhere near feeling what she felt to begin with?

Which was a big if, she reminded herself.

Brenda tried in vain to shake off the thought. This was all transitory, she silently insisted. It would be over before she knew it.

But before it was…

But before it was she wanted to savor it, to enjoy what she could. Because this was her one shot. There was no question in her mind that it was. She knew that in her soul. Until he'd come along, she'd almost given up believing it was possible to feel like this. Even if that shot missed, she'd have memories and at bottom, that was all they all had. Memories.

"Hungry?"

She had a feeling that wasn't the first time he'd asked her just now. She focused her mind and nodded. A change of subject to something nice and neutral was good. "How about pizza?"

He was about to make the suggestion himself. "No more craving for French fries?" he teased.

She looked at him sharply. Craving was just a word he'd pulled out of the air. "No," she teased back. "I've decided to switch cravings to pizza."

"Then pizza it is."

As he entered the early evening flow of traffic, he eased back on the gas. Taking out his cell phone, he punched a single number and checked in with the two officers he'd left at the bus terminal. As expected, they had nothing new or positive to report. No one in the area remembered seeing a man in a Giants cap and jacket carrying two black bags. So much for getting a description of a possible getaway vehicle.

Suppressing his frustration, Dax told the men to go back to the precinct and see if any of the calls had yielded something for them to work with. He didn't hold out much hope there, either, but you never knew. Some of the biggest cases had been solved by accident, because of something that had nothing to do with the case in the first place. The pieces were all out there, he just had to find them and place them in their proper order.

For the moment, as far as the case went, they were gridlocked. He had an uneasy feeling there was something he was missing, a piece that wasn't fitting in with the rest, but for the life of him, he couldn't see it from this perspective.

He needed his batteries recharged. Dinner might help.

Making a decision, Dax drove up to a restaurant that was known throughout the area for its pizza. This was where you went when you wanted to indulge in some serious pizza-eating. Pulling into the lot, he paused a moment after cutting off the engine and looked at Brenda.

"To go?"

Eating dinner here would be safer. But she didn't want to be safe. Not tonight. Tonight she wanted to be with him. Even more than she wanted the pizza.

She smiled in response to his question. "To go."

* * *

Forty-five minutes later, they were in her apartment, on the floor, the box with its hot, bubbling pizza between them. To their credit, they ate some of it before other appetites rose to push the thought of food far into the background.

As he took her into his arms, Dax realized that he'd been waiting for this from the moment he'd woken up beside her this morning. Despite the case, despite everything he knew should come first, thoughts of being with her, of making love with her, had hovered in his mind through the course of the day. Another first.

Healthy, red-blooded with a finely tuned libido, Dax still knew how to put everything extraneous, everything that didn't pertain to his case, on hold whenever he was working. Up until now, it had all been compartmentalized. When he was working, those kind of thoughts, those kind of urges, just didn't enter into his working world.

But now they had. Entered into it like Caesar marching into Rome.

All he wanted was to be with her in every manner possible, make love with her until he couldn't draw a steady breath into his lungs.

Maybe even after that.

"I like the taste of pizza served this way," he told her, savoring it on her lips. He licked his own, then ran his tongue along hers again.

Her heart continued hammering. The deep kiss had almost sent her over the edge. It had certainly done a number on her pulse. And managed to blot out all thoughts of everything but him. The word "more" urgently echoed in her brain.

Her body quickening, moistening, she smiled as she wrapped her arms around his neck.

"Another serving coming up," she promised just before she pressed her mouth to his.

She could feel the urgency in his body, the desire that took hold of him instantly and gloried in the response she felt in her own. She could feel her body humming with anticipation, heating even as all he touched was her back as he pressed her closer to him.

And eagerness seized her, laced with a measure of fear.

What if last time had been an anomaly? What if it was only a one-time thing, heightened by her vulnerability and her need to be wanted?

But even as she worried, she could feel Dax working his magic, could feel the fear loosening its bonds from around her. In her heart, she knew he wouldn't disappoint her.

The man was a wizard, casting spells on her with his hands, with his mouth. With his body as it pressed against hers.

She couldn't wait.

Eagerness seized her, spurring her on. The moment he began to undress her, her fingers began to work the buttons out of their holes on his shirt, tugging it out of her pants. All the while, as she worked, their lips hardly broke contact and when they did, she was quick to reintroduce the connection again.

Her head was spinning and she loved it.

Loved him.

The single thought vibrated in her mind. She buried it immediately, afraid of what it might mean. Of where it could lead her.

Better to live for the moment.

He made her feel beautiful. As his fingers strummed along her skin, touching, caressing, fondling, he made her feel beautiful, like some exquisite piece of art fashioned just for him. Admired just by him.

She knew it was all an illusion, but he made her feel loved and for the space of a tiny eternity, she clung to it.

And as she did so, all the feverish sensations speeding through her body intensified. She realized that it was as if last night with him had been a dress rehearsal and now this was the real thing.

This was show time.

She could barely catch her breath, but even so, she wanted more. More of the wild rush she felt as he took her from one climax to the next, accomplishing it in a variety of ways she hadn't thought possible.

Dax found places at the side of her neck, in the hollow of her elbow, along the slope of her belly. Over and over again, the explosions came, seizing her in their grasp, making her sob his name. Tossing her between agony and ecstasy.

Next time, she promised herself, next time she'd

make him go out of his mind. But right now, he was doing it to her. Rocking her world, transforming it into a fourth of July celebration. It seemed that his primary concern was that he brought her pleasure. She adored him for that, too.

But what if, a tiny voice whispered in her head, there wasn't going to be a next time? What if this was it, the last time they would make love together?

The thought, the fear, spurred her on.

Summoning strength from some nether region she hadn't known she had access to, Brenda managed to flip their positions. The surprise on his face was worth the superhuman effort it had taken her.

He'd barely kept himself in check. Twice he'd wanted to enter her, to savor the ultimate moment with her, and yet he'd held off, wanting to please her. Wanting to blot out the memory of every other man she'd ever been with from her mind just as she'd blotted out the memory of every other woman from his. He didn't know where this was going, told himself to take it as it came, but in his heart, Dax knew that this was different. She was different. She mattered.

He held on to her hips as she fitted herself over him, then bit back a cry as she began to move them in a timeless rhythm that seized him.

"Damn, but you're beautiful," Dax murmured as he filled his hands with her hair and drew her down to him. He wanted the taste of her lips on his when the ultimate rush came.

And when, in the next heartbeat, it did, he knew

that he didn't want it to end. Didn't want to ever have to let her go.

The realization scared him, but at the same time, he knew that it felt right.

That she felt right.

Chapter 13

He didn't know he could be this happy.

As far back as he could remember, barring some momentary crisis or other, he'd always been a happy person. It was a natural state of being, coupled with the optimism that seemed a given within most of his family, immediate and extended.

But he'd never been happy, really happy with a capital H before.

It was as if wild bursts of sunshine went off in his bloodstream at unannounced moments and all he could do was sit back in awe of it, never knowing when the next one would hit. He was powerless to divert it, powerless to initiate it. But he could enjoy it.

And make love with Brenda again. Which he did. With all the passion and tenderness he could muster.

After the euphoria had settled deep into his bones the second time, Dax struggled to rouse himself rather than to give in to the very real temptation of staying the night with Brenda, holding her in his arms. The struggle was made more intense by the fact that his cell phone hadn't rung, which meant that none of the people working on the task force under him had anything they thought important enough to share with him.

A lazy contentment threatened to spill out through his body, claiming him. The scent of her hair seeped into his senses, seducing him. Dax dug his knuckles into the mattress, forcing himself into a sitting position. He had to get up before his resolve became the consistency of a fruit pop left out in the sun.

"Don't go," Brenda whispered, wrapping her fingers around his arm. Surprising him.

Dax laughed softly and leaned over to kiss the top of her head. "I thought you fell asleep."

She allowed herself a soulful sigh, making him think of a cat who had just eaten a saucer of cream. "Just resting." Her mouth curved as she looked up at him. Another salvo of sunshine went off in his veins. "Trying to get my strength back for another go 'round."

This time, the laugh was louder as he shook his head in wonder. "You're giving me a hell of a lot of credit here."

She took a deep breath, trying to draw herself out of the delicious half-asleep, half-awake state she was in. She could still feel the warmth of his skin beneath her cheek even though he'd gotten up. It excited her even as it spread a soothing blanket over her.

"I think you're up to it." And then she grinned, her eyes sparkling as they looked up into his. "No pun intended."

"Oh, I think you intended it." Grasping her shoulders, he bent over Brenda and just lightly brushed his lips over hers. Anything more and he knew he wouldn't be going anywhere. "I think you intend everything that happens."

She raised herself up on her elbow as he got up, trying not to be distracted by the sight of his naked body. She needed him to understand that this had just happened between them, that she hadn't attempted to orchestrate anything.

"Actually, no."

Her tone was so serious, he stopped to look at her over his shoulder. "Then you're as surprised as I am."

Without realizing it, she ran her tongue along her lips, savoring the taste of him and succeeding in exciting herself. "Completely."

"Nice." Doubling back, Dax allowed himself one more quick kiss, then got up again.

When he didn't head for the bathroom but the opposite direction, Brenda sat up in earnest. "Where are you going?"

"To get my clothes," he told her. "I'm going back to work."

It was almost eleven. She was secretly hoping he'd stay the night, the way he had the first time.

"Did someone call?" She didn't think she had dozed off after they made love, but it might have been possible. And if she had, then she would have missed his phone ringing.

"No," he called out from the living room. His clothes were scattered throughout the small area, along with hers. He slipped them on quickly. "I just want to go over everything from the beginning, see if there's anything I missed." Dressed, he walked into her kitchen. "But you completely drained me, woman. I need energy. Where do you keep the coffee filters?"

Coffee. It was the first thing she thought of when she needed energy herself. Brenda got out of bed. It was nice that they had things in common, even small things.

"In the cupboard above the counter," she called back to him. "The one closest to the sink." Brenda pulled on fresh underwear and slipped on a pair of jeans that were slung over the back of a chair. "If you give me a second, I can make it for you." When he made no answer, she wondered if he'd heard her. "Dax?"

She began to button her blouse when her initial directions echoed in her head. The cupboard above the sink.

That was where she kept the prenatal vitamins her doctor had issued her, a prescription because she needed the extra iron in them. She was in the kitchen before her thoughts had a chance to form completely.

The set of his shoulders as she saw his back told her it was too late. She could feel a large hole opening up in the pit of her stomach. Dax turned to face her, holding the bottle in his hand. His eyes were expressionless as they met hers. "What are these?"

His tone was very, very still.

A chill ran over her heart even as she told herself it was going to be all right, that she could make him understand.

A small voice inside her head whispered, no, you won't.

Brenda couldn't make her legs move forward. She stood frozen where she was, staring at him, her breath caught in her lungs. Finally, she managed to say, "They're prenatal vitamins."

He'd read that. Read the patient's name on the bottle as well. But he couldn't get himself to believe it. Didn't want to believe it. "Whose are they?"

She could lie, could make up some story about trying to pull a sleight of hand over on the insurance company for a friend or something like that. If ever there was a need for a lie, this was it. But she'd already committed the sin of omission by not telling him about the baby; she couldn't compound it now with a lie.

She drew a breath, trying to stabilize her shaky pulse. "Mine."

He looked at the date on the bottle. This wasn't an old prescription, she'd filled it less than a month ago. "You're pregnant?"

"Yes." The word burned in her throat as tears gathered in her eyes, anticipating what was to come.

The single word slammed into him with the force

of a block-long moving van barreling down the free-way. Pregnant, Brenda was pregnant. With someone else's child. He'd made love to her and all the while, she had been carrying someone else's baby.

"Why didn't you tell me?" he demanded, his anger barely contained.

The fact that she hadn't told him, hadn't said anything at all about the baby, stunned him even more than the fact that she was pregnant. Because it destroyed the illusion he'd allowed himself to build up that there was something special, something good and unique going on between them. How could there be when she'd kept something so important, so huge, from him? She didn't trust him.

Brenda remained where she was. It was only through extreme determination that she managed to hold herself together. If she took so much as one step forward, she was going to dissolve in tears. Her hormones felt as if they were ricocheting wildly all through her. "I didn't know how."

His expression hardened. "Very simple," he told her coldly. "You could have looked at me and said, 'Dax, there's just one little thing I need to tell you before we knock boots—I'm pregnant.'"

She stiffened at the harsh, cold image he painted. "I was afraid that if I told you I was pregnant, you wouldn't make love with me."

Anger filled every part of him, making him rage, making him unreasonable. He threw down the bottle. It bounced on the counter, then fell into the sink, still closed. "So that's why you didn't tell me? Because you were horny?"

"Don't say that," she snapped angrily. Vainly she tried to construct a wall around herself, a wall so that he couldn't hurt her. But it was too late. "You make it sound so cheap and it wasn't—not for me."

He laughed dryly, his eyes narrowing as he looked at her. How could he believe anything she said to him? "Right, the earth moved."

"Yeah, it did," she shouted at him. Her own anger allowed her to cross to him, to get into his face. How dare he doubt anything she felt? "For me. I've never been with anyone before my husband, so I'm not by any means experienced, but I thought that what I had with Wade was all there was." She was fighting tears now. He had to understand, he had to. "But you showed me there was more, so much more. I knew this was nothing special to you, the way it was to me, so it wouldn't matter to you whether I was pregnant or not."

Nothing special to him. Well, he couldn't very well admit that now, could he? Not without looking like more of a fool than he already felt he was. "Let me get this straight," he said coldly, pretending confusion. "If you thought it wouldn't matter to me that you were pregnant, why didn't you tell me?"

It was all so twisted, so confused in her head, she couldn't begin to untangle it. Brenda pressed her lips together. She had no answer for him.

And he had no words for her, none that he could trust himself to say out loud. Picking up his jacket off the rug in the living room, Dax walked out of her apartment without saying another word.

The door vibrated in his wake as he slammed it.

Brenda covered her mouth with her hands. Slowly she sank down on the floor and let the sobs pour out.

Dax didn't realize that he'd driven his car over to his father's house until he pulled up in the driveway. When he focused on his surroundings, he shook his head. It was as if there was some kind of a homing device within the car, if not within him.

For a moment, he remained in his car, letting the engine idle. Trying to decide just how many different kinds of a fool he was.

How could he have gotten so entangled in her in such a short amount of time? This wasn't him, wasn't the way he operated. Fast and loose, short and sweet, that summed up his love life heretofore. When something's not broken, you shouldn't mess with it.

But he had. Messed with it bad. Without ever intending to. When had his guard gone down? Why wasn't he even aware of it happening?

Damn it, he'd gotten broadsided without even realizing that he was operating a vehicle. That he had ventured out on the road again.

"You going to come in, or just sit there like some mesmerized mannequin, letting the car idle until it completely runs out of gas? Money burning a hole in your pocket, boy? They paying you too much these days?"

He looked up and saw his father at the rolled-down passenger window, looking into the vehicle. Looking at him.

The next moment, Brian Cavanaugh took the decision out of his son's hands. Going round the hood, he opened the driver's side door.

"Come on in, I just made some fresh coffee and as usual, I made too much." There was a rueful smile on his lips. Five years since the funeral and he was still making coffee for Dax's departed mom, expecting her to walk into the kitchen, rummaging for coffee. The kitchen had turned out to be his domain rather than that of the woman he'd married. "You know how I hate throwing things away."

A half smile formed on Dax's lips. Coffee had been what had set the ball rolling in the first place. He still hadn't had any. He nodded and got out of the car.

Talking to someone, keeping his thoughts occupied until he could pull himself together again, was better than sitting around and brooding. He didn't doubt that was why he'd subconsciously driven over.

He followed his father into the house where he and his brothers and sister had wreaked havoc not so long ago. Several coats of paint hid the fingerprints that somehow managed to liberally cover the walls despite all of his late mother's warnings to the contrary.

How much paint did he need to apply to hide the hurt, the anger, he was feeling right now?

He shut the thought away. Or tried to.

In the kitchen, Brian crossed to the coffeemaker

and got down two cups from the overhead cupboard. He lived alone now that the last of the kids were gone and, like his brother, didn't like it. Nothing pleased him more than having one or more of his kids drop by, even though he got to see them almost every day at the precinct.

He eyed his oldest born now. "This about the case?"

A million miles away, or, more to the point, ten, Dax blinked. "What?"

Brian nodded at his son. "That look on your face, you look lost in thought, as if you were surprised you showed up where you did. This about the Tyler case?"

"Yeah." And then, because other than the white lies that pockmarked every kid's childhood and had dotted his own, he'd never lied to his father, Dax changed his answer. "No."

Turning with the pot of coffee in his hand, Brian looked at his first born and recognized the expression on his face. It was the same expression he'd seen staring back at him in the mirror after he'd had a fight with his late wife.

"Oh, I see."

No one needed to tell him that his father was sharp. He took pride in that. But when it came to his father being smarter about his private life than he was, that was something else again. Dax stiffened, instantly on the defensive, as if his mistakes were something to be jealousy guarded instead of torpedoed out into the ocean. "See what?"

Brian allowed himself a smile. "I'm not chief of detectives because of my looks, boy." He shook his head as he poured an inky cup of coffee for Dax, then repeated the process for himself. The thicker the better had always been his belief. He didn't trust coffee that let him see the bottom of his cup, even for a moment.

"Was beginning to think I'd never live to see the day," Brian murmured, half to himself, as he replaced the coffee pot on the burner.

Dax was still on his guard. "Never live to see what day?"

Brian took a seat on the stool beside him at the breakfast-nook counter. "The day my son finally found someone who mattered."

Raising his cup, Dax put it down again without taking a drink. His father was too close to the subject. And dead wrong. "What the hell are you talking about?"

"The look on your face," Brian replied mildly. "It's the kind of look a man wears when the woman he loves has gotten to him." He tried to seem nonchalant as he asked, "Trouble in paradise, son?"

Dax set his mouth grimly. "No paradise, Dad."

"I know it feels that way now, but whatever it is, it'll blow over." His expression grew slightly more serious. "Just make sure you don't blow it."

Dax gritted his teeth together. Served him right for not paying attention and driving over here in the first place. He'd meant to go to the precinct; winding up at his father's house was by pure accident. "There is no woman, Dad."

Brian's face was the picture of innocence. "No?"
"No."

The old man always could see right through him,
Dax thought, only partially annoyed. He wondered if
it was a gift he'd been born with, or something that
happened when you had kids. Like a fairy godmother
granting you a super power to help you keep up with
over-energized younger people.

Dax relented. A little. "Just someone I met a couple of days ago."

The smile on Brian's face was knowing. "Time isn't
a factor, Dax. I knew an hour after I met your mother
that I was going to marry her, or live single the rest
of my life."

More fairy tales. Well, he was too old for that kind
of thing. "Not everyone's like you."

Brian inclined his head. "No, but there's more like
me than you think." He gave Dax's shoulder a reassuring squeeze. "Whatever it is, you'll work it out.
I've got faith in you. You've got a good head on your
shoulders, Dax, you always have."

Too bad he didn't have any faith in himself, Dax
thought as he took a long sip of coffee. Choking it
down, he could almost feel it land in his stomach. His
eyes watered slightly as he looked at his father. "God,
what is this, dad? It tastes like boiled mud."

Brian beamed with pride. "My own special brew.
Want more?"

Dax pushed his cup forward on the counter. "Yes,
please."

* * *

Brenda dragged her hand through her hair. She felt like hell on a bad day. She'd spent the entire night trying to find ten minutes of sleep and had only half succeeded.

In reality, she was too exhausted to go to work, but in no condition to remain home, alone with her thoughts and staring at the walls in her apartment. And though she wanted to go, there was no way she could just show up at the Tylers.

Simon Tyler had made it abundantly clear that he didn't want her there and she knew after last night, Dax wouldn't appreciate the sight of her either. Even though the kidnapper had demanded to talk to only her, she doubted very much if either Tyler or Dax would be calling her to talk to him. The kidnapper had what he wanted.

But, on the outside chance that she was wrong, she made sure her cell phone was on as she put it in her purse. Staying home, waiting for God only knew what, was out of the question. She knew she would literally go out of her mind.

She had no other choice but to go to work.

She showered quickly, keeping the phone close by, then dressed and left. It was only after she was on the main thoroughfare driving to the academy that she remembered she'd forgotten to take her prenatal vitamins. She might as well have kept them in the medicine cabinet, she thought ruefully. At least then Dax wouldn't have found them.

It was better this way, she told herself. Deception was nothing to build a relationship on. And now, there was no relationship to build.

She forced her mind on her job. And remembered that when she'd called Matthew about not coming in yesterday, she'd told him that she'd be gone today as well. He probably had a substitute in place. But plans could change, right? Look how much her life had changed in the last few days.

Stop it, she ordered silently, turning up the radio in her car to drown out her thoughts. She couldn't afford to go there yet. She'd fall apart if she did. The only way she was going to make it through the day was if she didn't think, just acted. Automatic pilot was a state she was more than familiar with. She'd been on it more than once in her life, most recently the day she'd found out that she was a widow and a mother within an hour.

That which doesn't kill us makes us strong.

She didn't feel particularly strong right now.

She knocked lightly on Harwood's door, then stuck in her head. "Hi."

Matthew seemed surprised to see her. "I didn't think you were coming in. Is there anything new?" The words rushed out.

Yes, there's something new. I fell in love and got dumped, all in under a week.

"No," she told him. "The police are still trying to find leads."

He looked pale to her. She wasn't accustomed to

seeing him this way. He was normally so poised, so at ease with every situation. The kidnapping had taken a definite toll on him.

"I know I told you I wasn't coming in, but I thought I might do some good here."

He nodded. "Of course. I'm glad you're back. The children have missed you."

And she'd missed them, she thought. They were what kept her grounded and right now, she desperately needed that.

Walking into her classroom, she nodded at the substitute who had been called in.

"No, stay," she urged as the woman silently took her cue and began to gather her things. "I have a feeling I might need help today."

Instantly, the children were around her, leaving their desks and firing questions at her. For once, she allowed order to take a back seat. They'd been through a lot by proxy. Counselors were still on standby.

"Did they find Annie?" a little redhead asked her eagerly.

More than anything, she wished she could say yes. "No, not yet. But they will."

"Did the bad people really take her?" a little boy wanted to know.

"No, Tommy, they didn't," Alicia, her most vocal student, chimed in. "Mr. Harwood wouldn't let them take her."

Brenda smiled. It was wonderful to have such faith, to be so young and feel so protected. "Mr. Harwood wouldn't have wanted them to take her, but he wasn't there to stop them, Alicia."

Alicia frowned, her small blond eyebrows drawing together. "Why not? He took Annie out of line."

Something tightened within Brenda's chest. She remembered hearing Matthew tell the detective that he hadn't seen Annie on the day she was kidnapped.

Without trying to frighten the little girl, Brenda turned toward her and crouched down to her level. "When, Alicia? Think very carefully now. When did Mr. Harwood take Annie out of line?"

Alicia raised her chin. "I don't have to think carefully. I remember. It was when the fire alarm went off."

Chapter 14

Brenda stared at the little girl, her mind racing, entertaining thoughts that couldn't possibly be true. Alicia had to be mistaken. Matthew Harwood was dedicated to his school. He loved children. There was nothing else in his life. He wouldn't do something as heinous as be involved in Annie's kidnapping.

But if so, why had he lied to the police about not seeing Annie?

Brenda struggled to keep the urgency out of her voice. She didn't want to alarm Alicia, although the little girl had a fearless aura around her. It was one of the reasons she'd attempted to couple her with Annie in the first place, hoping some of that courage would rub off on the latter.

Her eyes held Alicia's. "Alicia, are you very, very

sure? Maybe you're confused about when you saw him with Annie."

The children around them fell silent as they listened in rapt attention. Alicia remained adamant. She nodded her head so hard her silken blond hair bobbed up and down around her small shoulders.

"It was after the fire alarm rang. We were running out of the art room. Annie was behind me and I turned around to take her hand—you said we were supposed to have partners," Alicia reminded her.

"Yes, I did." Brenda forced a smile to her lips, encouraging Alicia to continue. All the while, her mind was reeling. If this was true, then Matthew really was mixed up in this somehow. "Alicia, why didn't you say anything about this before?"

Alicia looked surprised at the question. "Nobody asked me if Mr. Harwood was with her."

No, Brenda thought, they hadn't.

She had to find out for herself.

Rising, Brenda looked at the substitute who was clearly confused by what was going on. That made two of them. And there wasn't time for explanations, even if she could pull one together that would satisfy them both. She needed more.

Brenda crossed to the door. "Would you take over the class, please?"

"Of course," the substitute replied.

"Aw." Nineteen small voices converged, becoming one in their protest.

She stopped to look at the upturned faces. Any one

of them could have been kidnapped instead of Annie. They didn't realize how lucky they were.

"I'll be back," she promised them.

Halfway down the hall to Harwood's office, she stopped abruptly. As much as she wanted to confront the headmaster, as much as she wanted him to give her some kind of plausible explanation for what Alicia had seen and tell her why he'd lied about seeing Annie, she knew she had to hold back. Going into his office now with this would lose the element of surprise.

If they needed it, she amended.

In her heart, she knew what she had to do. She had to call Dax.

Instantly, she felt a weakness wash over her. She didn't have that luxury, she argued silently. This wasn't personal, this was about saving Annie.

Making a U-turn, she ducked into the recreation area.

This hour of the morning, the large room with its big screen TV—ironically a gift from Simon Tyler and his wife—and entertainment enhancements was empty. She didn't want anyone overhearing her make her call.

While dialing Dax's cell phone number, Brenda's stomach felt as if it was twisting into a very tight knot. As it rang against her ear, she mentally counted to ten in an effort to get herself under control. Her nerves refused to cooperate.

And then she heard him, heard his deep voice as it echoed against her ear. "Cavanaugh."

Words rushed into her head. Why did you leave like that? Why didn't you come back? Why didn't you talk to me? She forced them all back. Now wasn't the time. Maybe it never would be.

"Dax, I think you should get down to the school." She heard silence on the other end of the line and wondered if the connection had gone dead. "Dax, are you still there? This is Brenda. You need to—"

"I know who it is."

His voice was distant, each word measured out. An awkwardness threatened to swallow her whole. But this was bigger than her feelings and the relationship that had been so abruptly aborted; it had left her reeling.

"Listen to me," she ordered. "According to one of my kids, Harwood took Annie out of line just before we left the building during that fire incident. I heard him tell you he hadn't seen Annie that morning."

"How much imagination does this kid have?"

"Her parents are both scientists. She is as pragmatic as a six-year-old can be. More."

"Where are you right now?"

"I'm at the school right now. I came into work because…" She caught herself in time. "Because the school was open."

He didn't question her. Despite his talk with his father, he wasn't up to discussing what was going on between them just yet. Only that he knew it couldn't be over this way. But that was for later. "Have you said anything to Harwood?"

"No, not yet."

"Don't." She thought she heard a hint of approval in his voice, but that could have just been wishful thinking. "I'll be right there."

She was left with a dial tone in her ear.

Brenda was on the steps waiting for him when he pulled up in the parking lot shortly thereafter. She looked wan, he thought, as if someone had kicked apart her world. That made two of them.

He resisted the temptation to say something to her. To touch her face the way he wanted to. Instead, he asked about the girl. Brenda took him to her immediately.

He thought it best not to remove Alicia from the classroom, but to question her apart from the others. The substitute herded the rest of the children, their curiosity severely peaked, to the other side to play a learning game.

Brenda gently ushered the girl forward. "Alicia, this is Detective Dax. He'd like to ask you some questions."

Alicia looked up at him. "I remember. You came here after the fire."

He felt as if he was talking to an intelligent adult instead of a six-year-old child. At six, he was playing with his cousins and getting dirty. The little girl before him looked as if she was preparing to do long division. In her head.

"Yes, I did. Do you want to tell me what you told Mrs. York?"

Alicia tossed her head, sighed and repeated what she'd said earlier. "Mrs. York was getting us out of the art room. Annie was behind me. I turned around to take her hand because Mrs. York always wanted me to be friends with her and I saw Mr. Harwood taking Annie away. He was holding her by the hand and talking to her. She was smiling." She'd uttered the entire statement on one breath and huffed as she came to the end of it. Getting a second wind, she looked up at the detective. "Okay?"

Dax nodded. "Okay," he repeated. And maybe, just maybe, he thought, things were okay for the first time since the kidnapping case had begun. He smiled down at the girl. "Thanks, Alice."

"Alicia," the little girl corrected with an indignant sniff.

Brenda bent down to the girl's level. "He's not good with names," she confided, looking at Dax. "You can go join the rest of the class," she told her, nodding at the other end of the room.

Alicia hurried off to see what she had missed so far.

Matthew Harwood jumped when Dax and Brenda entered the room. Had he not been sitting behind his desk, Dax had the impression the man would have sank onto something. He looked clearly shaken to see them unannounced.

Dax had warned the secretary to remain where she was just before he'd walked in on the headmaster. You could tell a lot about a person caught off guard.

"Detective Cavanaugh," Harwood greeted him nervously. "Any leads?"

Dax didn't bother wasting time with idle chatter. He was having trouble controlling his temper as it was. "Mind telling me why you lied?"

Harwood's pale complexion turned even paler. "I beg your pardon?"

Brenda couldn't hold back any longer. "Alicia Maxwell told us she saw you taking Annie Tyler in the opposite direction of the entrance when we were evacuating the children out of the building because of the fire alarm."

Dax's face was completely stony as he added the final nail into the coffin. "You told us you hadn't seen her that morning."

Harwood began to draw short, shallow breaths. "I was mistaken. With everything that happened, I got confused."

Dax didn't need any finely honed instincts to tell him that the man was lying. Harwood's very state testified to that. "Get unconfused," Dax ordered.

Harwood's dark brown eyes shifted from Dax to Brenda and then back again like tiny marbles in search of a place to rest. It was as if Alicia's unwitting observation was the last straw, overburdening a mind that was already on the brink of snapping.

He broke down in front of them, dropping his head in his hands as he struggled to keep back a sob. His world, already cracking, now shattered right before his eyes. When he looked up again, his eyes were wild and pleading for understanding.

"She wasn't supposed to be hurt. She was never supposed to be in any danger."

Dax restrained himself from hauling the man up to his feet and shaking him. "Then you did take her."

"No, they did," Harwood cried. "I just lured her away from the others, told her it was a shortcut out, I had her wait in the gym until they came for her."

"They?" Dax demanded.

"The Jamisons, Jim and Cloe." Harwood looked at Brenda. "That's their real name, not Kingsley."

"That's the name they gave you," Dax corrected coldly. He sincerely doubted the couple had used their real name. More and more, they were beginning to seem like professionals who had hooked up with Harwood in order to use his connections for personal gain.

Harwood knotted his fingers together, staring at the single spot on his desk blotter. "I don't know how this happened. Please, you've got to believe me, it wasn't supposed to be this way."

"Why don't you start at the beginning?" Dax told him. "And talk fast." Every minute they spent here was a minute they lost in recovering Annie. He just prayed it wasn't already too late.

Ashamed of what he had done, knowing that the path that had led him to this desperate act was no excuse, Harwood lowered his eyes again. "The school's been in financial trouble for a long time. I—I wasn't as careful with the finances as I should have been."

The man was being euphemistic. Dax cut through the rhetoric. "You gambled away your money."

Harwood's head jerked up, surprise written on his face. He'd tried to be so careful. No one was supposed to know. "How did you know that?"

"I looked into some things." It had been what he was working on this morning when Brenda had called. When looking at a dead end, he'd learned to approach the problem from another angle. Harwood had been the other angle. "You were in debt pretty badly."

Stunned, Brenda could only look on and listen. There had been rumors that the school needed to cut back, that mounting expenses made it difficult to maintain the high quality they had up until now, but she had no idea it was because Harwood was gambling away his money. No one even knew that Harwood went to gambling resorts, much less was addicted to them.

The man looked as if he was aging visibly right before her eyes as he made his confession. "The school was going to have to shut its doors, I was going to go bankrupt. They were going to take my house...I was desperate."

Dax prodded the man along. "How did you get mixed up with the 'Jamisons?'"

Harwood took a deep breath. "I met them in Tahoe. At Caesars Palace." He licked his lips, trying to push the words out. "I'd just had a streak of incredibly bad luck, lost more than I could ever afford to lose. I was at the bar, trying to think of what I could do, getting pretty plastered I guess," he admitted ruefully. "This couple sat down next to me and started talking. They were very sympathetic, said they knew what it was like to be on a losing streak. We talked for a while, I told them about the school, they seemed to be familiar with it. Somewhere along the line, I forget just when, Jim said he had an idea that might just help all of us."

"I just bet he did," Dax said grimly. He leaned over the man. "Whose idea was it to take Annie and hold her for ransom?"

Matthew scrubbed his hand over his face, trying to pull the events of that fuzzy night into focus. "Jim's," he finally remembered. "He said the daughter of a big-time producer like Tyler would get me as much money as I needed to pull myself out of debt and help get the school back up on its feet."

Dax looked at Brenda. His theory was right. He'd felt it in his gut all along. He took no joy in it. "They played you, Harwood."

Confusion creased Harwood's face, deepening the lines already there. "Played me?"

"They didn't just find you by chance, they went looking for you," Brenda broke in. How could he? How could he have risked the life of a child to help cover up his own weaknesses, his own mistakes? She wanted to grab him by his shirt and shake him. "Detective Cavanaugh had a hunch that this was an elaborate plan to get back at Simon Tyler for something, as well as get the money."

"I—I don't know what to say. I'm so, so sorry."

"Not good enough, Harwood," Dax snapped. "When are you suppose to get in contact with them?"

"I was supposed to get in contact with them last night." He sounded as if he was trying vainly to keep from babbling. "Right after they got the money."

Last night had come and gone and Harwood had looked like a man facing his own firing squad when they had walked in just now. "But?" Dax demanded.

Harwood looked close to tears. "But I can't reach them. No one's answering the phone. I went over this morning, but they're not there."

Dax exchanged glances with Brenda. It was getting to look very, very bad. "Where's there?"

Digging into his pocket, he produced a folded sheet of paper with the name and address of a motel. Underneath was the cell phone number that "Jim" had given him. "They said they'd be staying there until this was over," he offered. "They're from Los Angeles."

Well, at least that tallied, Dax thought. He asked what he felt in his bones was a useless question, but then, one never knew. Sometimes even the smartest criminals did stupid things. "Did they give you an L.A. address?"

Harwood shook his head as guilt entered his features. "I never thought to ask."

"It probably would have been bogus, anyway," Brenda pointed out.

"Probably," Dax agreed.

Hysteria began to fill Harwood's voice. "You have to understand." Again, he addressed his words first to Brenda, then to the detective, "I was desperate. I was going to lose the school, my house, everything."

Dax looked at him coldly. "I'd say you've already lost it."

Without another word, he turned from the man and took out his cell phone. He needed an officer to come down and take Harwood away.

Harwood turned to Brenda, begging for absolution. When she began to turn away from him, he grabbed her arm. "I was desperate," he repeated, his voice cracking.

"And what do you think Annie is now? If she's even alive," Brenda shouted at him. Disgusted with Harwood, she shook the man off. "She's a little girl, Matthew. How could you?"

"I don't know, I don't know." Harwood buried his face in his hands and began to sob.

Dax flipped his cell phone closed, returning to them. "Someone'll be here in five minutes to take you down to the precinct," he told the man. "You can consider yourself under arrest."

Without feeling, he recited the familiar words that encompassed the man's rights. Harwood looked as if he barely heard them.

Not wanting to wait, Dax handcuffed the headmaster to his chair. "That'll hold you until they arrive." Even as he said it, the faint sound of a siren was heard in the distance. With a grim nod, Dax began to walk out of the office.

One step behind him, Brenda followed him out past

a stunned-looking secretary. "Where are you going?" Brenda asked.

Taking out Harwood's sheet, he held it up. "To the motel. Maybe I'll get lucky." He still had the sketches Brenda had done in his pocket. Maybe if he showed them to the motel manager, he would jar the man or woman's memory.

Preoccupied, it took him a minute to realize that Brenda had lengthened her stride and fallen into step beside him. "Where do you think you're going?"

There was no hesitation on her part. "I'm going with you."

"No, you're not."

"You can shout all you want, I'm still going."

Without giving her a backward glance, he strode out the door. A patrolman was just pulling into the parking lot. Getting out of his car, he hurried up the steps.

"He's in the headmaster's office," Dax told the policeman. "Handcuffed to his chair." He gave the man his keys. "I want those back later." With that, he continued down the stairs.

Brenda followed him, refusing to be put off. "Look, I just gave you a big break on this." She trailed him to his car. "I could have gone to Harwood myself, but I didn't. I called you first. You owe me."

At his car, he threw open the driver's side, then stared at her for a long moment over the vehicle's roof. Finally, he shrugged. Maybe brainstorming with her while they drove would prove useful. All he knew was that he didn't have time to waste arguing.

"C'mon."

He didn't have to say it twice.

"Give me that piece of paper," she said to him once they were on their way. "The one Matthew gave you with the cell number on it."

He dug into his breast pocket, holding it out to her as he drove through an intersection. "Harwood already said they weren't answering."

She took out her cell, carefully punching in the numbers that were meticulously written down on the sheet. How could a man who was so neat, who seemed so careful in everything he did, mess his life up so badly? It didn't seem possible.

"Maybe, but it can't hurt to try again, can it? Who knows, maybe one of them'll slip up and answer. If they do, you could tie the signal in, couldn't you?"

"I'd have to call into the precinct first, have them track it from there." It was a shaky idea at best, but he gave her points for trying. "The good news is that the precinct can track it via the wireless provider."

Brenda frowned. If they needed to call the precinct first, there was no point in trying to get someone on the line now. She was about to disconnect when she heard a voice answering on the other end of the line.

Exchanging looks with Dax, she placed the earpiece next to her ear. "Hello?"

"Hello? God, is that you?"

The voice was gravelly. It sounded nothing like the

man who had been in her classroom several days ago. "Who is this?"

"Jake. Jake the Prophet. Don't you know me, God? You told me to be out here."

Because she was willing to play any long shot, she asked, "Where's here, Jake?"

There was a long pause, as if the man on the other end was looking around, trying to find a landmark. "Katella and somethin'. I can't read it. Why don't you just look down and see? Oh-oh, gotta go." The line went dead.

Frustrated, she closed the phone.

Dax looked at her. "Well?"

She drew the most likely conclusion she could. "From the sound of it, I'd say they threw the phone away and some homeless person picked it up. Calls himself Jake the Prophet and he's somewhere along Katella, thinking that God uses a cell phone."

A half smile twisted his lips. "Who's to say?" Dax murmured as he took a shortcut to the motel.

The motel was located in a run-down part of town where people came and went without making eye contact and no one knew anyone else. It had been chosen for a reason, Dax thought as he parked his car in the uneven parking lot.

When confronted with the two sketches that Dax showed the motel manager, who obviously had no use for the police by the way he looked at Dax's badge, claimed not to recognize either person depicted until threatened with obstruction of justice.

That loosened his tongue. "Yeah, yeah, they were here, but they checked out."

"Did they have a little girl with them?" Brenda asked eagerly. She showed him Annie's photograph, but the man was shaking his head before he even looked at it.

"Not that I saw." He shifted accusing eyes toward Dax. "They stiffed me."

Every shred of evidence could be important. "They didn't pay?" Dax asked

Uttering a curse, the man laughed humorously. "Oh, they paid all right. With a credit card. Except that it bounced this morning. I ran it through when they registered, but the jerk on the night desk forgot to make sure it was still good last night. This morning, when I did it, I found out the account's been closed."

Dax held out his hand. "Give me the number."

Brenda looked around his shoulder as he dialed a number that would connect him to the credit card company. "What good is that going to do?"

"You'll see."

After he identified himself and gave the supervisor he'd been connected to his badge number, he was told the reason for the ban. The credit card had been reported stolen yesterday.

"All right, listen very carefully," Dax instructed the woman. "I need you to lift that ban for a few hours. We think the people who stole the card are responsible for kidnapping a little girl. Right now, the card is the only lead we have in order to track them. If we get lucky, they're going to try to use it again and soon. Call me at this number the second they do." He gave the woman his cell phone number.

"Now what?" Brenda asked as he flipped the phone shut and put it away.

This was the hard part. "Now we wait."

Chapter 15

Dax led the way outside. "You want to go somewhere and grab a cup of coffee?"

She felt the tension closing in on her again. Tension because of Annie. Tension because of Dax. She grabbed at anything that could hold it at bay even a second longer. "Might as well. There's no point in standing around here."

There was a coffee shop less than two miles away from the motel. They drove over. The morning was sunny, with a humid haze beginning to settle on the city.

Picking up the two containers he'd ordered, Dax turned to face her. "You want to stay inside?"

Somehow, that felt too confining. She needed space.

Brenda indicated a small table with an umbrella located a few feet away from the entrance.

"Outside." She glanced at the jacket pocket where he kept his phone. "The signal'll be stronger." It was as good an excuse as any.

"Right." Shouldering open the door, Dax followed her to the table. As far as he was concerned, the signal was already strong, at least the one that was prompting him to be with her.

To his surprise, when he'd asked her what she wanted, she'd ordered the decaffeinated coffee. He noticed the face she'd unconsciously made as she took a sip after sitting down. He'd seen less pained expressions on people who'd swallowed sour milk.

"That good, huh?"

Setting the container on the table, she regarded it with less than affection. "It's like drinking hot water with a brown crayon in it."

His own was a double espresso, guaranteed to bring all the hairs on his body to attention. To him, there was no reason to drink coffee if there was no caffeine in it. "You're not supposed to have caffeine?"

She lifted a shoulder in a half shrug. Studies reversed themselves, depending on the month they were done. "Doctors keep changing their minds about that. I figure I might as well be safe than sorry." She paused to take another sip. It was no better than the first. She stiffened to stifle a shiver. "Oh, well, at least it's not forever."

He took a long sip of his espresso, letting the thick

liquid pour itself through his veins. "You should have been honest with me, you know."

She raised her eyes to his face in that way that always seemed to make his stomach throw itself voluntarily into a knot. "Guilty as charged, Your Honor."

He had no idea where the sudden wave of impatience came from. He did his best to bank it down. "Then if you know that, why didn't you tell me?"

She pushed the container away. The bottom caught on something uneven on the surface and nearly tipped over. She caught it just in time. It didn't improve her mood. "Just how was I supposed to work it into the conversation? 'What's your favorite kind of baby carriage, Dax? And, oh yes, by the way, I'm pregnant.'"

"No," he said, just managing to keep his tone civil. "But you should have said something." He paused, gathering himself together, then looked at her. Faults and all, he still wanted her. "Is it Wade's?"

One look at his face told her he wasn't trying to insult her. Just being a cop, gathering facts to sort out at will. "You have to ask?"

He blew out a breath. When had life, his life, gotten so damn complicated? "No, I guess not. Did he know?"

She shook her head. "No, I found out I was going to be a mother and a widow all on the same day. Just hours apart," she added quietly. There was a sadness within her, battling to take over. She refused to let it. "Look, I couldn't find the proper way to tell you without making it sound as if I was assuming that this—this thing," she said for lack of a proper term, "between us was becoming a relationship and that it was going somewhere."

His eyes never left her face as she spoke. Dax knew that for the first time in his life, he wanted a relationship to go somewhere. He wanted it to go all the way up to the altar and beyond.

But he couldn't just put himself out there without her giving him some indication that she had strong feelings for him.

"Do you want it to go somewhere?" he finally asked.

Yes, damn it, yes!

The words hovered on her tongue, begging for release. But she was too afraid of making a fool of herself. She'd already experienced the pain of rejection because of him. What if after he had all the facts laid before him, it turned out that he didn't feel the same way about her that she did about him? Then what? She couldn't be asked to bleed twice. Last night had been enough.

"That's up to you," she replied, her voice devoid of all emotion.

When he didn't say anything immediately, she knew she had her answer. And that answer was that he didn't want a relationship, that he was only asking so that he could know, not so that he could respond in kind.

She felt tears closing in on her again. She picked up the container and took another sip in self defense. Anything to get her mind away from the pain infiltrating through her.

"Brenda—"

But as he reached for her, his cell phone rang. Dax immediately shifted gears. He pulled his phone to his ear as Brenda watched, her eyes wide and hopeful.

"Cavanaugh. Wait, just a minute, give me that location again." He grabbed a napkin, then felt his pockets for a pen. Brenda produced one out of her purse. Nodding at her, he quickly jotted down the address the person on the other end was reciting to him. Thank God criminals slipped up. "Thanks. If they use the card again, I want to know." He slapped the cell phone lid closed. "That was the credit card company. Our kidnappers just used the card. We've got a location."

She was on her feet instantly, her adrenaline rushing. "Where?"

"Gas station, twenty miles from here." Leaving the last of his espresso, he hurried to his vehicle. "Maybe they had to clean up some old business," he speculated.

Something inside of Brenda froze. "I just hope that 'old business' wasn't Annie." Beyond that, she wouldn't allow her mind to venture.

Inside the car, Dax was on the phone again, alerting Nathan to this latest kidnapper sighting and giving him the address of the gas station.

"I want five people there to fan out in the area," he said as he drove out of the small strip mall parking lot. "If there're any sketches left of the couple or flyers with Annie on them, bring them with you."

Closing the phone, he put it away again. As he did so, he glanced at Brenda's face. "What are you doing?"

"Praying."

"Yeah," he muttered, looking back on the road. "Me, too."

The gas station attendant identified the man in the sketch after some hemming and hawing coupled with head scratching and only after Brenda had added a mustache.

"Yeah, he was here. But he was alone."

"Which means," Dax said to Nathan who had arrived on the scene less than a couple of minutes earlier, "that he's left his partner and the girl somewhere, most likely at a motel."

Nathan frowned as he covertly slanted a look toward Brenda. "Or he's ditched them both."

They both knew he didn't mean the word ditched. It was a euphemism to spare Brenda's feelings until the very end. "Let's hope it's the former." Walking away from the attendant, Dax's mind kicked into high gear. "We need a list of all the motels in the area," he told Nathan. "They've been splattered all over the media, he's not going to risk checking into an upscale hotel with Annie."

If Annie's even with them, Brenda thought, hurrying along in their wake.

They were about to question their third motel manager when Dax's cell phone rang again. Emotionally worn out, Brenda immediately crossed her fingers as he answered.

The conversation was short, ending with Dax murmuring, "Must be karma," as he hung up.

"What is?"

"That was the credit card company. The woman there said the card was just used at the Blue Bird Motel, not more than fifteen minutes ago."

She raised her eyes. The faded sign above the manager's office, a tiny building sadly in need of paint, proclaimed the establishment to be the Blue Bird Motel. "That's this place."

"Bingo."

Stopping, Dax was hitting numbers on his keypad again, calling in his people. They had a target now.

Two minutes later, he was leading the way into the less than pristine manager's office.

"Morning, folks, what'll it be?" Dressed in a T-shirt that proclaimed the name of a new band on its way up, the young man behind the counter was barely out of his teens. On his thin face he sported what he probably hoped would pass for the beginning of a goatee. Dax estimated that a turtle had more hair on its back. "Only got a few rooms left," the clerk was saying. "Season's a busy one."

Dax held up his shield. The clerk paled visibly. His breathing grew dangerously shallow. "Did I do something wrong?"

"No, why would you think that?" All sorts of possible tie-ins went through his head. Was this kid involved in the kidnapping, too, somehow?

The young man looked trapped as he stared down

at the dirty blotter on the desk. "I only added ten to the price of the room, honest. He looked like he could pay it." When his head bobbed up, there was contrition written all over his face. "But I'll give it back, I swear and I'll never do it again." Dark eyes shifted back and forth between him and Brenda. "Jeez, how did you guys find out?"

Dax played along, looking for some kind of leverage in obtaining the man's cooperation. He'd learned that if you let someone talk long enough, you're bound to get something on them.

"We're the police, we know everything." He dug into his pocket, producing the sketches. "These two people come in here wanting a room?"

Appearing to be more than a little petrified, the clerk looked from one sketch to the other. "Maybe. I'm not that good with faces. But the mustache looks familiar and if you made her hair darker…"

Disguises. He'd expected as much, Dax thought. "What room did you give them?"

"One-two-oh." The clerk spat the number out. "Why, are they in some kind of trouble, too?"

Brenda pushed her way to the counter. "Was there a little girl with them?"

But the clerk shook his head, his stringy hair waving back and forth. "I didn't see no little girl."

The words cut through her heart. Did that mean…?

"Oh God, Dax."

Dax said nothing, just gave her hand a quick, reassuring squeeze even though he felt far from confident himself. The couple had their money, they didn't need the little girl anymore. That meant they could have disposed of her at any time. Which put them in a brand new category.

Murderers.

"You got the key?" Dax demanded.

The clerk nearly fell over himself as he got a spare out of a rectangular grouping of cubbyholes with hand painted numbers above them. The key shook as he held it out to him.

Nathan and the others hadn't arrived yet, but Dax felt he couldn't afford to wait for them. Every second counted in a situation like this.

He also knew he could rely on Brenda to stay in the car, so he decided to use her.

"Tell them you're the maid bringing them towels," he instructed as they hurried across a weed-covered courtyard. "And once the door's opened, I want you out of the way." He pinned her with a hard look. "Understood?"

"Understood," she echoed. She only half heard him. Annie had to be with them, she had to. People didn't just kill little girls in cold blood, they didn't. It was more of a prayer than anything else.

Once at the door marked 120, Dax drew out his service weapon and pointed to Brenda.

She knocked once, then again.

"Yeah?" A thick voice demanded from inside the room.

"Housekeeping, sir. I have towels."

"We've got towels. Go away."

She exchanged looks with Dax. She tried again. "Please, sir, it's my job. The manager'll fire me if I don't give you these towels."

"All right, all right, give me the freakin' towels," the man growled as he threw open the door. The next second, he was staring down the barrel of a gun. "Run, Cloe," he yelled as he tried to slam the door again.

Dax pushed the door all the way open. "Freeze," he ordered. "You're under arrest."

The sound of approaching sirens mingled with screams and shouts from within the room.

"Where is she?" Moving from behind Dax, Brenda shouted at blonde woman. "Where's Annie?" When Cloe said nothing, Brenda stepped forward, as if to force it out of the woman's throat. "I said where's Annie? Tell me where she is or I swear I'll—"

"Mrs. York? Mrs. York!" a muffled voice from the closet cried.

Instantly, Brenda turned from the woman, rushing to the closet. Behind her, she was vaguely aware that the police had entered the room. From the sound of it, two of them took the woman prisoner.

Brenda threw open the closet door and her heart caught in her throat. She sank to her knees. Annie was inside the barren enclosure, tied up and blindfolded. There was a gag around her mouth as well, but she'd somehow managed to work it loose.

With shaking hands, Brenda quickly undid the

blindfold, then the ropes. The little girl squinted against the light.

Brenda gathered her into her arms, holding the little girl close, fighting her own tears. "Annie, oh Annie, you're all right. It's all over, baby. You're going home."

Annie said nothing, her face wet with tears. She clung to Brenda as if she would never let her go, wrapping her arms and legs around her like a gibbon monkey.

Brenda remained kneeling as she kissed the top of Annie's head over and over again, murmuring soothing words. She felt Dax's hand on her shoulder as she rocked with the little girl.

There were no words to express the depth of Simon Tyler's gratitude. To everyone's surprise, he dissolved into tears beside his wife as Dax and Brenda brought his daughter to him at the mansion.

And when he'd managed to pull himself together, in an unprecedented show of generosity, he wrote a huge donation to the police department on the spot.

He gave the check to Dax. "So that you can buy the department state of the art computers and programs like the one she used to help find Annie." He nodded at Brenda.

"I'll pass it along," Dax promised. He felt tired and wired at the same time. The case was over. Nathan had taken the two suspects down to the precinct in order to book them. Matthew Harwood was already down there, cooling his heels in a cell.

He turned toward Brenda and gestured at the Tylers. "Why don't we leave them alone for now?"

Brenda merely nodded.

"Looks like it's all over but the shouting," he said as they left the mansion. And then he looked at her, admiration in his eyes. "Speaking of shouting, you were some wildcat back at the motel. I thought I told you to stay back once the door was open." He couldn't even muster a pretense at annoyance. In her place, he would have done the same thing.

"Sorry, slipped my mind." She felt tired, drained and relieved. But there was a glow that was missing. This was going to be the last time that they saw each other. The realization weighed heavily on her. "Can I get a ride from you? My car's still in the school parking lot." And then she laughed softly to herself, although the sound had little humor in it.

Taking her arm, he brought her back to his car. "What's so funny?"

"Nothing, it's just that this'll probably be the last time my car'll be there." A sadness drifted through her. She'd been at the academy for three years and had grown to love it. "The school will be closing down without Matthew to run it. That means I'm out of a job."

Was that the only reason for that sadness he detected? "I wouldn't worry."

She looked at him, trying to gauge his tone. "Why?"

"I've got a feeling that once that computer equipment Tyler's funding arrives at the precinct, the department's going to need someone good to help teach the rest of us bozos what to do with it. Most likely, they'll want to keep you on, too, to help with the hard stuff, so I don't think you need to hit the bricks just yet, looking for a job."

His words, he noted, seemed to comfort her a little. She was unconsciously running her hand along her stomach. Something he'd seen countless other expec tant mothers do, he couldn't help thinking.

Dax held the door open for her and then closed it after she got in. Moving around to the other side, he slipped in behind the wheel.

Now or never, he thought.

Leaving his keys in the ignition, he turned toward her. "Now that that's out of the way, you and I have some unfinished business."

"We do?"

"We do. Back at the coffee shop, you asked me a question."

She remembered. She'd thought he'd answered it with his silence. "I did?"

"All this excitement make you forget?" He sincerely doubted it. The lady was too bright for that. Was she not-so-subtly telling him to drop it? He was in too deep; he couldn't. His natural sense of self-preservation took a back seat to something that was now consuming him. His need for her. "You asked me if I wanted our relationship to go somewhere." He paused, waiting for her to say something. When she didn't, he forced himself to get the words out. "I do."

She could feel her pulse accelerating. "And where is it you want it to go?"

He took another cautious step along the tightrope. Below him was a sheer drop, but he had no choice. He had to do this. Had to let her know what he felt. In hopes that she felt it, too.

"Does the 'sky's the limit' mean anything to you?"

Don't hope, don't hope, you know how disappointed you get when things don't work out the way you want them to. You already know that life isn't a fairy tale. She took a deep breath before answering. "It's a term people use when betting."

"And I'm betting everything, putting it all on the line."

She shook her head. "I lost you."

He took her hand in his. Her fingers felt cold. Was she nervous? He began to feel better. Because he was nervous as hell.

"That's just it, you didn't. Look, I'm not sure how to say this, so I'm just going to say it straight out."

Fairy tale, her mind mocked her. She clung to the edges of it anyway. "'This?'"

Like a swimmer about to dive into ice cold water, he braced himself. Then jumped. "I love you and I want to marry you."

The words had rushed at her like a speeding train. She stared at him, not sure she'd heard what she'd heard. The mind played tricks, sometimes. "Why do I get the feeling you just read me my rights?"

"The only rights I'm concerned with right now is

your right to say no." Dax searched her eyes. "I'm hoping you won't exercise it."

Brenda smiled at him and he could feel the rays begin to enter his soul. "Why would I say no when everything inside of me is shouting yes? In case you hadn't noticed, I love you, you big stupid jerk."

"I love it when you talk sexy like that."

Her smile continued to fill him until it spread all the way through his being, just the way it had the first time he had made love to her. He had a feeling it was there to stay.

Which, he thought as he brought his mouth down to hers, was just fine with him.

Epilogue

Faye Walker had been a nurse for close to thirty years. She'd worked maternity for twenty of those years, most of them right here at Aurora General. She had seen a crowd scene the likes of which was presently engulfing the waiting room only once before. And it had involved the same family.

That birth had taken place less than three months ago, when Maggi Cavanaugh had presented a darkly handsome, widely beaming Detective Patrick Cavanaugh with a healthy baby girl.

It looked like history had just repeated itself, same scenario, different players.

She surveyed the area. There wasn't a place left to sit and almost no place to stand. Obviously anyone named Cavanaugh didn't remotely believe in the virtues of practicing abstinence.

Faye Walker cleared her throat. Instantly, like a wave in the ocean, the people within the room moved toward her. A formidable woman standing almost six feet with girth to match, she held up her hand as if to physically dismiss the questions that were about to come her way.

"Two," the woman announced, holding up the same amount of fingers and slowly passing her hand before the crowd of siblings, father, uncle, aunt, cousins and assorted mates. "I'll take two visitors in at a time. And just two," she warned.

Troy began to move forward when Jared pulled him back. "Dad and Janelle," he told his younger brother, making the choice for everyone.

Troy, always the impatient one, inclined his head and sank back into the multitude. "But I get to go next," he announced grudgingly.

Following the nurse, Janelle and her father slipped quietly into the birthing room where, only minutes before, Brenda had been going through the soul wrenching agony of bringing a new life into the world.

"You look great, kiddo," Brian said to her.

Wanly, she smiled her thanks. "Never felt better," she murmured.

Dax was standing beside his wife, looking far more relieved than she did. Brian knew how that felt. Childbirth was still a miracle, but things went wrong with miracles sometimes. He had held his breath each time his own wife had gone through this. Being here, waiting for his first grandchild to be born had brought it all back to him.

"What's her name?" Janelle asked softly as she looked at the precious being wrapped in a pink-and-white receiving blanket and nestled in the crook of Brenda's arm.

"Elizabeth. Elizabeth York Cavanaugh," Dax said. "We named her after Mom."

"She's beautiful," Janelle whispered. There were tears in her eyes as she looked up at her brother.

"Why shouldn't she be?" Brian asked, laying his hand on his daughter's shoulder. "She's a Cavanaugh, isn't she?"

Dax exchanged looks with his father, gratitude in his eyes. It didn't matter that the child his wife was holding hadn't had his blood at the very start; she had his heart now.

Miss Elizabeth York Cavanaugh was family and, ultimately, that was all that mattered.

* * * * *

FAMOUS FAMILIES

YES! Please send me the *Famous Families* collection featuring the Fortunes, the Bravos, the McCabes and the Cavanaughs. This collection will begin with 3 FREE BOOKS and 2 FREE GIFTS in my very first shipment— and more valuable free gifts will follow! My books will arrive in 8 monthly shipments until I have the entire 51-book *Famous Families* collection. I will receive 2-3 free books in each shipment and I will pay just $4.49 U.S./$5.39 CDN for each of the other 4 books in each shipment, plus $2.99 for shipping and handling.* If I decide to keep the entire collection, I'll only have paid for 32 books because 19 books are free. I understand that accepting the 3 free books and gifts places me under no obligation to buy anything. I can always return a shipment and cancel at any time. My free books and gifts are mine to keep no matter what I decide.

268 HCN 9971   468 HCN 9971

Name	(PLEASE PRINT)	
Address		Apt. #
City	State/Prov.	Zip/Postal Code

Signature (if under 18, a parent or guardian must sign)

Mail to the **Reader Service:**
IN U.S.A.: P.O. Box 1867, Buffalo, NY 14240-1867
IN CANADA: P.O. Box 609, Fort Erie, Ontario L2A 5X3